WICKED HUNGER

Burgundy's Story

SHADOW SISTERS
BOOK IV

CHLOE ADLER

Signum Publishing

Copyright

WICKED HUNGER BY CHLOE ADLER

Book 4 - the final book in the Series: Shadow Sisters
This book was previously published as A Vampire's Wicked Hunger and Overcome.

Join Chloe's Newsletter and grab a FREE Novella!
Fire and Fangs is a sexy, enemies to lovers, multiple
partner/why choose paranormal with sword-crossing.
***https://BookHip.com/QFGLCWZ

ISBN: 978-1-947156-07-4
Copyright © 2017 by Signum Publishing
Cover: 2023 Rebeca Covers ©
Editor: Elizabeth Nover - Razor Sharp Editing

Also by Chloe Adler

Shadow Sisters

Mortal Desire, Dark Craving, Fevered Heart, Wicked Hunger

Tales From the Edge

Distant Light, Radiant Light, Blazing Light

Chronicles of Tara

Synergist, Planeswalker, Keystone

Destiny Chronicles

Descent, Dedicated, Devotion

Danger After Dark

Paris, Venice, Barcelona, London

Chapter One

A warm breeze rustled through the acacia tree outside, carrying the scents of fall through my partially cracked window. Rex and I were dozing on my bed, languidly enjoying the morning. It was one of the advantages of having a night job. A familiar knock sounded, the handle turning. Jared didn't need to be invited in. He had free rein.

"Good morning, Miss Burgundy Rosales." He was carrying a bamboo tray laden with two cups of coffee.

I sat up in bed, the velvet comforter slipping down to my waist. I didn't bother covering my bare breasts. It was warm enough, and neither Rex nor Jared would care. I patted the space next to me. He handed me the tray, piled up a few pillows and propped himself against my lavish headboard, careful to avoid disturbing a sleeping Rex.

Jared sighed, taking his cup off the tray. "I love our morning ritual. And your room."

"Your room is just as nice in a different way," I countered. Jared Weks had fastidious tastes and had become my best friend the instant we'd met four years ago. He'd shown up one day outside the V Club with nothing more than a backpack and a look on his face like someone had just slaughtered his family, which was probably because . . . they had.

Nor was Jared the last stray I'd adopted. When I'd brought a spunky, red-haired witch home a couple of months later, Sadie Holt had claimed both our hearts. We were all still extremely close. I couldn't imagine that ever changing. Even after Sadie had met Ryder and Jared had met Alec, they were still my closest friends and occasional lovers—Sadie more than Jared because, well, Jared was gay. My tastes, however, were a little more . . . fluid.

Besides, I had Rex now. As if he'd heard my unspoken thoughts, Rex perked up out of his nap. He raised his head from my lap and gave my nose a delicate lick.

Rex really was the perfect man. Minus the four legs, the doggy slobber and the need for someone to pick up his poop. I scratched his head as his tail thumped happily against my leg. Oof, that tail packed quite a wallop, attached as it was to his 110-pound Rottweiler body.

"What happened last night?" Jared blew on his coffee.

Oh yes, last night. Since he worked part-time at the same club I did, there was nothing I could hide from him. Not that I wanted to hide anything. "I could ask you the same question."

"You're the one who disappeared into one of the back rooms. Spill. I want to hear all the juicy details."

Though the V in V Club stood for vampire, all Signum were welcome there—vampires, shifters and witches. Plus humans. The V was a combination bar, dance, strip and sex club, but a lot of people just went to drink and dance. It was one of the few places in Distant Edge open twenty-four hours. We stopped serving alcohol at two a.m. because, well, that was the law in California, but the place stayed open around the clock.

I playfully punched him in the shoulder. "One of my tasty donors was in town. She stopped by so I could feed."

Vampires only needed to feed once a week. We could even go longer if we were willing to sacrifice some of our extraordinary strength and speed, but not me. I held too much too close. Most vampires rotated morsels so we didn't feed from the same human more than once a month. For those vampires who were gorgeous or even just entertaining, the supply of donors was endless. Vampires often had waiting lists. I certainly did. But for the stragglers or the assholes, blood could be more difficult to acquire, and it usually required cash. Luckily, there was at least one vectum per town—bars in which vampires could pay humans for a bite. One forward-thinking entrepreneur had even started a mobile vectum. Like a food truck, except no one but vampires would order their virgin Bloody Marys.

"I thought you looked particularly flushed this morning." He leaned in and kissed my cheek.

"Thank you." I batted my lashes at him. It never hurt to practice. "Where's Alec?"

"Still asleep. He had a late night too."

"I noticed." I ran my tongue slowly over my full lips. Alec danced at the V, but his act was less stripper and more Chinese acrobat, bringing people far and wide to drool over his . . . skills. Alec had recently started training at the local circus too.

My phone rang.

Jared picked it up off the bed. "It's your father."

"What?" I snatched it out of his hand so quickly he gave me a hurt look. I offered him a shrug and a smile. He knew how much my father meant to me.

"Dad. Hi, is everything okay?"

Jared moved to the foot of my bed to give me one of his famous foot massages, and I sank back into the pillows.

"Baby girl," my dad purred in my ear.

I was over forty and he still called me that. It warmed my heart. Probably because vampires and witches aged differently than humans and shifters did. I didn't look a day over twenty-five, yet he still cherished the memories of my childhood.

"What's up?" I asked him. "You haven't called in weeks. I was starting to worry."

"I'm in love, what can I say?" he responded. "Margery keeps me busy, and we're creating a life together."

I sighed. My dad had left my mother several months earlier and though my mother was devastated, my father was happier and more vibrant than I'd ever seen him. "I'm happy that you're happy, Papa."

"I don't think I've ever been happier." His voice practically beamed.

Ouch.

"I can't wait for you to meet her," he gushed. "And her daughter, Deenie. You're going to love them both. As much as I do."

"I'm sure I will." I wanted to. My dad's happiness was paramount to me, even if it did remind me of everything I didn't have.

Jared looked up from his perch, raising one eyebrow at me. I shook my head at him and he went back to work on my feet, expertly pressing and kneading. I stifled a moan.

My father's voice rose an octave as he pulled the phone away from his mouth. "One minute, sweetheart, I'm on the phone."

"Can you come visit soon?" I asked.

"I'd love to, pumpkin, as soon as things settle down here. Margery is working on a big case right now and needs my support." His voice lowered to a whisper. "How is your mother?"

"She's upset, Dad."

"Naturally." His voice turned stern. "She'll get over it and see it was for the best."

"I don't know . . ." My mother was not a strong woman.

His voice altered again as he held the phone away. *"Si, si, mi amor."*

I waited.

"I've got to go, Maria. I love you. I'll call again when I can."

"I love—" But he'd already hung up.

Chapter Two

An hour later we all sat at the kitchen table. Jared, Alec and I were drinking our morning coffee. Chrys—Sadie's witchy sister and my other roommate—was drinking tea, and her disgustingly gorgeous boyfriend Carter was drinking nothing. He, too, was a vampire, but he only drank blood. Not me. I couldn't resist human food, and all the wasted calories had given me the voluptuous figure to prove it.

For vampires, human food was nothing but junk food. We put on weight if we ate it, but I'd never cared about that, nor had I ever gotten any complaints from my many lovers or the patrons who watched me dance at the V.

"What does your dad's new girlfriend do?" asked Chrys.

"My mom told me she's a divorce lawyer." I sighed

into my coffee. "And apparently she's a really good one too."

"She's not your dad's lawyer, is she?" asked Carter.

"No, but someone else at her firm is."

"Is that legal?"

"In Nicaragua it is."

"But didn't your mom say that he was cheating on her?" asked Jared.

I nodded. "That's what she suspects, but my dad would never do that. It must be easier for my mother to believe he's the bad guy. Plus you know how over-sensitive she gets. So easily riled."

"And yet," said Jared, "he is living with this woman only a few months after he left your mother."

"I don't think he knows how to be alone. Some people just like to feel taken care of and needed. I think the timing and the fact that she works in that law firm are coincidental." I'd never lived by myself either. Though it was starting to look like I would soon. Here I was, in my early forties and still alone while my closest friends were all hooked up and in love. *Stop this ridiculous internal drama; you have the perfect life.*

"Isn't your dad a lawyer too?" asked Alec.

"Yeah." I got up from the table to pour myself more coffee. "But he's a Signum-civil-rights lawyer and his girlfriend's firm are divorce lawyers."

"Well, maybe they met in court," Chrys shrugged, "or at the courthouse."

"So what's everyone got planned for today?" I asked, purposely changing the subject. The last thing I needed was for my friends to suspect my father was something he most certainly was not.

"We were going to walk down to the boardwalk with Rex," said Jared.

"Want to come with?" asked Alec.

"Sure."

Rex trotted alongside as we headed toward the boardwalk. It was only a mile from my house, Casa Mañana, and the walk was lovely. Breezy but not too cold. Southern California had a way of remaining temperate the whole year round, unlike the hotbox I'd grown up in, Granada.

"Nice outfit." Alec grinned at me as I held Rex at a heel.

I was a fashionista, no denying it. Probably because of my Taurean nature or maybe because my mother was not. I almost always donned tight-fitting skirts or dresses that hugged every curve, many made of velvet. Plus the cleavage was on full display. Why not flaunt it if I've got it? And if people got so hung up on the surface they didn't dig deeper, all the better.

Walking onto the pier, I was looking at my favorite storefront and all their bling when I hit something solid. Hands reached out to steady me.

"Burgundy," said my employer in his clipped British accent.

"Benedict."

The vampire scared pretty much everyone except for me. I appreciated how forthright and businesslike he conducted himself. He bent down to pet Rex and I waved the boys on.

"I'll catch up with you in a minute," I called after them. Addressing Benedict, "Everything okay at the club?"

"Everything's fine there." He stood and locked his menacing gaze on me. "It's the Council."

I waited. He also resided on the city's Council and was usually transparent with me about their goings-on. He slicked back his already slicked-back, dark hair. "There are some uppity humans, and I proposed hiring a Signum-civil-rights attorney."

My eyebrows shot up. "You know my dad is one?"

He nodded. "I do. I was wondering if he could recommend someone in San Diego County."

"I can ask him but, well, why not offer the job to him?"

"Doesn't he live and practice in Central America?"

"He does." I licked my lips. "However, things are changing for him at the moment, and it's always been my dream to have him live in Distant Edge with me."

"Could work." Benedict straightened his sunglasses. "He'd still have to pass the bar here first though."

"Already has. He has his license to practice in three US states as well as Nicaragua and Spain."

Benedict cocked an eyebrow at me.

"He's good at what he does and has been working around the world for decades."

"That I don't doubt. Everyone's heard of him, he has quite the reputation, but rumor is he has quite a high fee because of it."

"Yes, but he doesn't need the money anymore. The man's a billionaire. I can ask him. Maybe he'll volunteer just to be close to his little girl." I flashed Benedict a smile.

"Let me know. I'll see you later tonight." He threw me a curt nod and walked off.

"That would be a dream come true," I cooed to Rex. He licked my hand in response. "Come on, let's find the boys."

They were standing in line at the Harbor House Cafe, our favorite breakfast spot, and Jared was on the phone.

"Anything amiss?" asked Alec.

"All good." I wasn't one to gossip but I was nosy. "Who's Jared talking to?"

"The girls. Sadie called. He's trying to convince them to join us."

Good thing it was a Saturday, which meant Sadie was off work. Her new landscaping business was thriving, even after just a few months. I'd invested my entire savings to help her and I couldn't be prouder of my BFF. In a year, she'd be making enough to start paying me back. *But then what?* a little part of my psyche nagged, sinking its fangs into my neck. What would happen after she paid me back? She had her mate. She had a great new career. She'd no longer need *me*. But I wanted her to succeed. Didn't I? I was happy that my two closest friends had found their mates. Wasn't I?

"Iphi too?" I asked.

"Yeah, she's still sleeping on the couch there."

"I wish she'd move in with us instead. We can easily make room for her. Sadie only has the one bedroom."

"She's been talking about returning to Aurelia's soon."

Iphi was Sadie and Chrys's nineteen-year-old witchy younger sister. Their mother, Aurelia, was a very controlling woman. But now that she had started getting serious with Carter's grandfather, she was mellowing. Although she still scorned Chrys, who had been the favorite, for turning her into a toad back at the beginning of the year.

Jared clicked off his phone. "The girls are on their way."

"Should we call Chrys and Carter too?" I asked.

"Already texted them," said Alec, holding up his phone.

We had to wait a little longer for a large outdoor table, which worked out well since we also had to wait for everyone's arrival.

"So, anything new?" I asked Iphi when we were seated.

"Yeah." She pushed a flaxen curl out of her bright-blue eyes. "Mom's practically begging me to move back in and . . ." She chanced a look over at Sadie, who was busily talking to her other sister. "I'm not very comfortable at Sadie's." Redness flooded her cheeks. "I mean, I'm not a prude or anything, but I'm also not as," her eyes floated upward, "*open* as Sadie."

Sadie was a sesso, a sex witch, and she needed constant orgasms to access her powers. The other two sisters did not. Sadie's insatiable appetite had kept her in a state of distress for most of her life, but when she'd finally discovered who she truly was, the woman had blossomed.

"Is living there uncomfortable for you?" The question made me wonder how Chrys was faring at *my* house. She was much more of a moralist than Iphi, and yet I often brought lovers home.

"It would be fine if I had my own bedroom." Her cheeks reddened again. "I'm happy that Sadie and Ryder invite guests into their bed. I think it's kind of cool, but . . ."

"But?"

"You know, Burg," she lowered her voice, "I'm not that experienced and I mostly end up feeling like a third wheel. Er, I guess I mean a fourth wheel. Or fifth, depending." She giggled.

"That makes sense. Is there anywhere you can go when they 'partake'?"

"I sit out in the garden a lot or on the front porch, but sometimes they wake me up at night with their, um, festivities." Red cheeks again.

"Sounds like you'd be more comfortable back home, but my house is always open to you too."

"Thank you." She offered me a dimpled smile. The girl looked like a Botticelli painting. "But I think I'd have the same problem there."

"Probably." I laughed, bending down to pet the dog reclining at our feet.

Sadie leaned over. "Whatcha two laughing about?"

"Wouldn't you like to know," I leered.

"Nothing." Iphi's pale skin resembled that of a tomato.

Sadie clapped gleefully. "Iphi, you never could lie,

and by the color of your face, I'd venture you've touched on my favorite subject."

Chrys looked over from her seat. "Hey now, leave Iphigenia alone."

Iphi waved her hand at Chrys. "Thank you, big sis, but I'm fine down here." Then she leaned into my ear and whispered, "I don't mind talking about it one-on-one, but I'm not comfortable in a group, and I'm much less comfortable talking about my sister doing it, let alone hearing her."

"I get it. Makes perfect sense. So go back to Aurelia's for now. We'll figure something out."

"Mom is much happier nowadays . . ."

A tall, stunning black woman walked by our table. Iphi kept talking but her voice just stopped registering.

I'd never seen this woman in the Edge before. What deliciousness was beneath that long, embroidered coat? The bright colors reminded me of a Christmas present and I had to clamp my mouth shut to keep from gawking. That was a present I'd like to unwrap. Slowly. Button by button. I imagined revealing her delicate skin inch by delicious inch.

Obviously she liked clothes as much as I did, but that garment was more suited for Big Bear in January than the Edge in October. Did she hail from an even warmer climate? If her face and hair were any indication, that figure must be exquisite. She strolled to a table where an equally hot man waited.

In contrast, he was wearing significantly less clothing, only shorts and a wife-beater tank. He had wild, curling, blond hair with tendrils skewed haphazardly over his tanned forehead. She reached out and straightened one of his curls. When she let go, it boinged right back into place. He grabbed her wrist and she giggled. The man looked like a surfer or a beach bum with crystalline-blue eyes and long, almost white, lashes. His bulging biceps were dusted with freckles. He pulled her into him playfully and she planted a kiss on his cheek. Yum. Who were *they*?

Iphi's waving hand in my face broke the tableau. "Earth to Burgundy!"

Chapter Three

L ater that night I drove Jared, Carter and myself to the V in my 1976 red Camaro. Her name was Cherry. We were all working, which was rare since Jared spent so much of his time attending chiropractic college in San Diego proper.

"I'll just write this paycheck over to you," Jared said, looking over at me from the passenger seat.

"Not a chance," I replied huffily.

"Burg, I haven't paid a dime toward rent in months."

"When you're making bank as a chiro, you can start paying rent again. Save your paychecks for food, gas and schoolbooks."

"Yeah, man, it's not like a few hundred bucks will cover it anyway," said Carter from the back seat. "And speaking of . . . I'd like to contribute something. I practically live there now, and with Chrys in school I know she can't contribute."

"I knew Chrys couldn't afford rent when I asked her to move in last January. This is all on me, guys. It's my house."

"Wow, it's paid off?" Alec asked.

"Not your worry," I said, not unkindly. "It's taken care of. If I was struggling, that'd be a different story." I did not discuss my finances with my friends. My father was wealthy enough to help me out and I didn't want to foster any resentment. He had offered to buy me Casa Mañana, for which I was extremely grateful. And I had learned long ago to accept such gifts from him with grace. Jared was the only one who knew he'd helped and he was sworn to secrecy.

"Alec can help," Jared said. "He wants to pay his share and can afford to."

"I'd really like to as well," said Carter again.

"Please, men, no more talk of finances." My voice was stern. It was the tone I used to let people know a matter was no longer up for discussion. It always worked.

They collectively sighed but shut their mouths.

When we arrived at the club I went straight to my dressing room to change. There was a group greenroom but since I was the most senior dancer, both in age and in start date, I had my own. Before

Alec I was also the dancer who'd drawn the biggest crowd.

My room was furnished similarly to my house, with my favorite Moroccan decor. Again I blamed my astrological sign for my love of rich, sensual velvets and brightly colored brocades. I had splurged on the intricate, hand-carved, Balinese teak, four-poster bed. When I'd seen it in an import store in San Diego, I hadn't thought twice. It was during times like that my privilege showed. Where furniture and decor was concerned, I didn't hold back. Nor did I when it came to clothing or feeding my friends. I told myself it wasn't because I was entitled, it was because I came from money and made plenty of it on my own. Why shouldn't we all have the best? Within reason.

Sitting down in front of my black, wooden vanity, also elaborately carved, I reapplied my makeup. I never left the house without wearing a layer of foundation, mascara, eyeliner and lipstick, but for the club I had to add even more. My signature colors were red and, of course, burgundy, and my lips and nails were always painted to match accordingly. At this time of year, as we drew closer to Beltane and Yule, I favored red.

There was a brisk knock on my door.

"Come in," I said hesitantly.

It creaked open and Benedict poked his head in.

"Hey, Burgundy, is now a good time to introduce you to our new dancer?"

"As good as any." I returned to my makeup application, tracking the doorway in my periphery.

A dark woman with long, plaited hair walked in tentatively. I whipped my chair around, less to intimidate and more out of curiosity. Dancers came and went at the V but they were mostly white, so whenever a person of color joined our team, I was ecstatic.

However, the vision I was presented with almost knocked me completely out of my chair. It was the woman from the cafe. The word "stunning" did not do this woman justice. She was, perhaps, the most beautiful woman I'd ever seen and I'd seen a lot of women—up close and personal.

Benedict cleared his throat. "Burgundy, I'd like you to meet Tiyah."

I leapt out of my chair to shake her hand, which she had extended toward me. It was slender, with lovely long fingers, and warm to the touch. Human.

"Tiyah." I was at a loss for words, which had never happened to me before. I've been surrounded by beautiful people, especially here at the V. I had oodles of handsome men and lovely women throw themselves at my feet. Sometimes I tasted and other times not. Because the fact was, no one really moved me.

This woman moved me.

She gazed into my violet eyes, not removing her hand from mine and not speaking. Her own eyes were deep and basalt brown, like hardened lava hiding liquid magma beneath. Her lips were large like mine, but where my top lip was larger, hers nestled on the pillow of her bottom lip. I imagined taking those lips between mine and sucking hard or, better yet, biting them until I could taste her blood.

Benedict cleared his throat again, and she looked down, breaking eye contact, yet her hand remained in mine. "I'll leave you two to get acquainted." He didn't bother to hide the smile in his voice.

Neither one of us responded or turned to watch him leave.

Chapter Four

I was acutely aware that Tiyah was sitting in front of the stage to watch my routine. She had a lot of dancing experience but not "this kind" of dancing.

Entering as a sexy mad hatter—my favorite outfit —I paraded around on stage. My short, black, lace skirt stopped midthigh and the stiletto boots came up to my knees. I had on a tight bustier with a black and gold lamé fitted dinner jacket. The best part of the outfit, however, was the top hat. An oversized playing card was tucked into the band.

Although I often moved in similar styles, I always let my body feel its way through the music, picking the time it wanted to gyrate or sway. At certain beats I would swing on the pole or make eye contact with people in my audience, tossing my hair and licking my lips. The only part of the act that hit the same cues each time was the disrobing. It had to be perfectly timed so that by the end of the song I wore only my pasties and G-string.

This time, however, I couldn't take my eyes off that woman, and it wasn't until halfway through my act that I finally noticed the man sitting with her. It was the same blond, white surfer boy from earlier. When I moved my eyes from her to him, he shifted in his seat and put his arm around her, as though showing me she was his property.

Whatever. I could have anyone I wanted in the Edge and beyond. Humans traveled near and far to watch me dance and beg me to snack on them. Turning my attention elsewhere, I finished my set, making sure to end up near her so she could get a very good look at my almost-naked body.

The bar was crowded when I returned twenty minutes later, wearing my long velvet robe, but Jared had saved a seat for me.

"Great set." He smiled, placing a Michter's single-barrel bourbon in front of me. Jared knew all my favorites.

"Thanks." I leaned over the bar. "Hey, did you see the new girl yet?"

"New girl?"

"The new dancer that Benedict just hired, Tiyah. She's from Jamaica."

He shook his head. "Nah, but you know me. If

they don't have a cock 'n' balls, they're pretty much invisible to me." He winked and then jutted his chin to the opposite end of the bar. "Like that guy. I noticed him."

There sat the very surfer boy who had been manhandling Tiyah. He held his drink up to me, offering me a curt nod.

"He's with her, I think." I rolled my eyes at Jared. "The good ones are always taken."

"Ain't that the truth." He grinned, turning his head toward the stage, where his own man was entering.

A hand on my shoulder almost made me jump. I was pleasantly surprised to find that it was Tiyah's hand.

"My husband wants to meet you," she said, pointing to where he sat. "Is that okay?"

Crap, they were *married*? Life was just not fair. "Sure." I stood up and followed her over.

He extended his hand to me as Tiyah reclaimed her seat beside him. "Hi, I'm Elijah Aaron, Tiyah's old man." He grinned, his smile stretching all the way to his light-blue eyes. Twinkling and pale, they reminded me of moonlight shimmering on the surface of an ocean. "She told me how helpful you were earlier and I wanted to meet you."

"Elijah." I shook his hand.

"Here." He stood up, offering me his barstool.

I couldn't stop eyeing his sublime body but forced my gaze upward. That windblown hair, sun-kissed skin and boyish grin. Even though he truly did look like every surfer dude in San Diego, something in those sparkling eyes promised mischief. What a gorgeous pair he and Tiyah made. His white-blond curls towering over her delicious black tresses. Her honey-colored eyes to his sky-blue. The colors of summer and winter woven together. A Jamaican and a Jew. I loved that. Oh yes, he was a hottie indeed, inspiring just as many dirty thoughts as she did.

He, too, sized me up as they moved closer to talk over the noisy bar. Were they exclusive? Or swingers?

"So you're both new to Distant Edge?" I asked.

"We are," said Elijah.

Tiyah laughed nervously. "We officially moved here yesterday."

"What made you choose the Edge?" Most humans moved here because they were either enamored with the Signum or they were Signum-rights activists.

"I'm a divemaster," said Elijah, "working toward becoming a pro dive instructor in the US."

"There are a lot more opportunities outside the States," said Tiyah, "like Honduras or, well . . ."

"Practically anywhere else," he finished. "But I missed home, and Tiyah was willing to give In-N-Out and the NFL a try."

"He's a really good diver." Her voice was both high-pitched and sultry.

"Well, you certainly look the part," I offered.

Elijah laughed, which made me instantly like him. "Do you dive?" he asked.

"Nope. Not really my thing."

"Have you ever tried it?"

I ran my hands over my body. "Do I look like I've tried it?"

He shrugged. "Sure, why not?"

Tiyah leaned forward and squeezed my arm, all earnest appeal. "It's really fun. If you're game, we could take you."

Well, hell yes. Get next to them in a wet suit? Where do I sign up? "You could probably talk me into it." I winked at her.

"That would be great," Elijah said, but his brows drew together as his gaze dropped to Tiyah's hand. She pulled back as if burned, reaching for a glass on the bar top that contained more melted ice than liquor.

Jealousy? Not swingers then. "So where did you find a place?"

She giggled nervously. "We're currently on a boat in the Trinidad Marina."

"A boat boat, not a houseboat?"

"Right," he said. "It's thirty-eight feet and perfect

for the two of us." Was it just me, or had there been a certain emphasis on "two"?

I scrambled for a response. "Do you sail?" I'd always wanted to go sailing.

"We do," he said.

"Actually, the boat belongs to Elijah," she said, smiling.

Impressive, but wouldn't it belong to the both of them if they were married? "You have a gorgeous accent, Tiyah. You're from Jamaica?"

Her eyes lit up. "Jah."

"And you two met there?"

"I sailed there last summer to dive, saw her and fell hard. I couldn't come back home without her."

Nor could he bring her back here and have her work legally without marrying her.

"Aww, honey." She leaned in and kissed his cheek but her eyes were glued to mine.

Their vibe was all over the place. Poly? Or maybe she was bisexual and he let her play? I hoped she wasn't merely bi-curious.

She leaned toward me and I picked up the thick scent of fresh peaches. I could sink my fangs into her peach. *Focus*.

"So where do people go dancing in the Edge?" She waved her arm around. "Besides here."

"Yeah," he chimed in, "is there other nightlife? One would think, with so many Signum."

My dark mane bounced atop my shoulders. "The pier is the best place for nightlife. There are restaurants that stay open late and a fun ecstatic dance club called Promise. I often go there during the week. My favorite DJ spins on Wednesdays."

"Sounds *promising*." Elijah winked.

Tiyah clipped his shoulder.

"You forgot your drink," Jared said from behind the bar, handing it to me as I turned. "Anything for your friends?"

I introduced everyone and ordered another round —though not for me; I was thirsty for something else altogether. "It was great to meet you both." I slid off the stool.

Elijah reached out to touch my arm. "Can we get your number?"

My heart kicked over. Okay, maybe they *were* poly.

He leaned toward me, whispering in my ear, "It would be great for Tiyah. She's shy and needs friends here. Especially while I'm at work."

Argh, stupid heart. I did not need any more friends, but that woman intrigued me. "Sure." I grabbed the phone he was holding out and punched in my number. "See ya kids around."

Chapter Five

After work, sizzling with sexual frustration, I dialed up Sadie. The last thing I wanted was to pick up some random piece, but I needed to come and not alone. My entire body tingled at the thought of that woman, Tiyah—and if I let my mind go there, her husband too. Yum.

"It's so late. Is everything okay?" Sadie said when she answered, sleep in her voice.

"I need you and Ryder to fill my holes."

Sadie giggled. One of the many great things about your best friend being a sex witch was that she was up for it pretty much any time, even while she slept. "Hold on, let me check with my prince." Their voices were muffled before she came back on. "He says yes, but he also wants you to know that if it were a week-night, he wouldn't allow me to play."

"Understood. I'm on my way."

Their decorative fairy lights were blazing when I arrived a few minutes later. It was nice that the entire town of Distant Edge was not too big, unlike our neighbor, San Diego.

Sadie's cottage featured a wide front porch with modern patio furniture. The façade had been newly painted a pale blue. Again. By the ocean, paint peeled. Her front yard was also freshly landscaped, a la Sadie herself. No grass, because of the usual lack of water in Southern California, but gorgeous slate tiles led through a pebbled garden of succulents. Impressive. Both charming and professional. Several funky Asian brooms, handmade from grass, formed a sculptured centerpiece around her signage. Way to represent the witches as well as her new biz. I was happy to see she'd kept the two sycamores with the hammock in the side yard.

I let myself in with my key and locked it behind me.

"I'm here," I called out. No reason to startle. Her living-room lights were subdued, casting the walls in soft yellows. I looked around for Iphi, but she was nowhere to be seen.

"We're waiting for you in the bedroom," she called back.

I made my way there and knocked on their closed bedroom door.

"No need to knock," Sadie called out and I opened it to a lovely sight.

Sadie was already tied up, naked on their bed, and Ryder, also naked and kneeling beside her, was running a flogger gently across her reddening skin. I quickly closed the door behind me.

"Where's Iphi?" I asked, not wanting the innocent girl to hear us.

"Oh, she's probably outside." Sadie peered at me through heavy lids and licked her lips.

"What? She's here?"

"Yeah, but if you didn't see her in the house, she's probably hiding in the kitchen or in the backyard. She knows the drill by now."

"Doesn't it make you uncomfortable to make her uncomfortable?"

"She said she didn't mind," said Sadie. "Now get your delicious ass over here."

I snapped to attention. "You are not the one who gives orders," I hissed, but my tone did nothing to wipe the smile off her face.

I missed this. I missed what we *used* to have. I missed the time before Ryder, even though I loved him now too. But it had been different back then, when it had been just the three of us—Jared, Sadie and me.

I sauntered over slowly, letting my eyes graze over

Ryder's dark body. His skin shone in the dim lights like polished walnut. Utterly delicious.

"May I?" I asked him, approaching.

"Please," he murmured.

I walked behind him and ran my hands over his solid pecs, around his full biceps—where I paused to squeeze—and ever so slowly down his taut stomach until I fisted his hard cock. He groaned, leaning his head back against my chest.

Sadie's eyes glittered, watching. "I love it when you handle my man like that," she moaned.

"Shut up, Sadie, or I'll gag you."

She eyed me, knowing I always made good on my word.

"Suck him," she said.

Wow, she rarely defied me. I stood up, went over to her closet and removed a cotton scarf. Returning to the bed, I gently lifted her head and gagged my best friend, tying the knot snugly in the back. Then I pulled her hair hard, from the nape, the way she loved it. She strained and groaned through the gag. Reaching my hand between her legs, I dipped my fingers into her shaved pussy to feel the moisture gathered there, wetting her clit with her own juices and then diving inside her pussy. When she bucked into my hand, I stopped and bought my fingers to my mouth to taste.

"Delicious."

I moved back to Ryder, grabbing his cock again and teasing it with my hand. I leaned down and spat on it, getting it wet enough for my hand to slide. Tightening my grip, I squeezed upward, moving my fingers over the sensitive head before returning to the base. With my other hand I played with his balls, grabbing and tickling, then pulling. He groaned, fucking my fist while Sadie watched, writhing next to us on the bed.

I climbed onto the bed and faced him, sucking on his lips and jacking him hard. He yielded to me, his tongue exploring, one hand cupping my nape. His other hand worked its way under my skirts from behind and reached my wet cleft. They both knew what I liked but sometimes they teased. He pushed his fingers in and out, circling my clit, and then gently, using my own wetness, he pushed the tip of a finger into my ass. I clenched around him and his other hand dropped from my neck to lift the front of my skirts.

"I want to fuck you," he growled. "I want to fuck you and I want Sadie to watch."

"Not happening," I purred. "Play with my tits. Now." A surge of pleasure shot through me, reminiscent of the very first time all three of us had come together. When the power differential had been skewed in my favor. I was the one who had found Ryder for my bestie and brought him home to use.

He'd been the third wheel, before things had shifted. Before they'd fallen in love.

Immediately he complied with my request. They all did.

We moved over a little so Sadie could watch, her neck straining toward us, garbled moans escaping around the gag.

He pulled first one breast out of my bodice dress and then the other, and they spilled over the front as he dropped his head to suck. He took a nipple in his mouth and teased it with his tongue and teeth. Biting hard and then soft until it peaked, reaching for him. As he broke off to lick them, his eyes were locked on his woman's eyes. They loved watching each other. Compersion. Passionate polys. I craved what they had.

Ryder kept fingering my ass and expertly playing with my tits as my appetite grew. His cock was rock-hard in my hand and I tightened my grip even more as he pumped into it. He was close.

"Don't come yet," I growled. His hips froze midthrust, though he didn't look up from his task.

Letting go of him, I reached for the wet wipes on their bedside table and held one out to him. He stopped the tit play, removed his finger and wiped it off obligingly.

"Your turn to watch. You can pump yourself but you're not allowed to come. Understood?"

He nodded, reaching for his cock.

I gently climbed on top of Sadie and pulled the gag down. Her red hair was splayed over the white pillow in a halo of lust. Immediately she lifted her head, her mouth open and reaching for mine. I climbed up her body and dropped one of my tits into her mouth. She suckled deeply, pulling hard on my nipple.

I reached down between her legs and played lightly, strumming the very tips of my fingers over her outer lips. Her thighs went taut. When she tried to speak I pushed my breast into her face, shutting her up. Ryder was watching silently, still holding his glistening cock.

"Get the clips and some candles," I ordered him.

He jumped up, moving quickly to the black wooden chest at the foot of their bed. It opened with a creak and Sadie stiffened, her eyes going wide.

"That's right, my little nymphette," I cooed evilly. "And keep sucking."

Ryder returned with a set of nipple clips that had a chain running between them. Two steel clamps, a white candle and a lighter. I pulled my breast out of Sadie's mouth with a pop and ran my hands lightly along her arms, following them up to where Ryder had fixed them tightly to their metal headboard. I jutted my chin toward her body, and Ryder jumped up to clamp each of her nipples between the black rubber tips and then tighten each screw carefully. Sadie was being a good girl and keeping her mouth shut but we both knew the pressure she liked, and if she was bad, he would tighten them just a bit too much.

While he was busy at her breasts, I moved between her legs, which were spread open nicely, also bound at the ankles. I massaged up her inner thighs, squeezing and kneading, to take her mind off her lovely rack. When I reached her lips I tugged and pulled on them first with my finger and then with my teeth, rolling and pulling each one. She groaned loudly. I attached two metal clamps and tugged. Her head thrashed from side to side. Holding the clamps with one hand, I caught Ryder's eye and nodded. We both tugged while I fastened my mouth to her clit. She rolled, bucked and finally began screaming.

Pressing my face into her, I licked, sucked and pulled until she was on the verge of orgasm, her warm bud swelling in my mouth, and then I stopped. Ryder and I smiled at each other as he dropped the clips and bent over to kiss her.

While they made out he moved his body to the side, exposing her nakedness to me. I picked up the discarded flogger and started whipping. The gurgling sounds coming from their kisses told me all I needed to know. Avoiding her stomach, I flogged her breasts and thighs. As a Dominatrix, I was fully adept with most implements of bondage and submission. A snap of my wrist and she moaned. Another and she twisted her body. Many minutes later I surveyed my handiwork. She was lovely and flushed, sporting a lot of tender skin and some minor welts.

Time for the hot wax. Lighting the candle, I held it an inch above her body, letting it drip onto her heated skin.

"Ouch, what the fuck?" she screamed into Ryder's mouth because he wasn't letting her go.

"Is that any way to speak to the woman with the wax?" Some perverse part of me was enjoying her discomfort, more than I usually did as a Domme. Few of my play partners were pain sluts, nor did I often feel the need to dish it out. Sadist light. But here, with Sadie, part of me wanted to push her limits, take her somewhere I knew she and Ryder hadn't explored yet. Hear her screams. Lick her tears. Make her suffer for having a relationship I could only dream of. *For abandoning me.*

So here I was, hurting my bestie on purpose in some sick passive-aggressive expression of alienation.

As soon as the thought formed, I stopped and blew out the candle. Jesus, what was I doing?

"Let's fuck," I said to Ryder and he immediately stopped kissing her. I helped myself to a double-sided dildo in their trunk, some lube and a condom. She was wet enough, dripping even, so I pushed the dildo into her wet hole and her pussy swallowed it. I handed a condom and some lube to Ryder and then climbed on top of her again, straddling her, holding her gaze. Guiding the other side of the dildo inside of me, I raised my ass and motioned for Ryder to climb behind me, over her legs. I didn't want him in my pussy but he could ravage my ass. God knows I could use something to pound some sense into me, and Sadie could enjoy the compersion of her fiancé wetting his dick. He poured the lube onto my crevice, fingering it in. Reaching back, I led his rock-hard member to the entrance of my ass, easing him in while I played with my clit over the dildo.

Though Sadie and I had slept together for years, the three of us . . . not so much anymore. Sadie had assured me we would continue our regular trysts with Ryder, but he seemed to prefer including strangers. Even more so if those strangers were just passing through. I couldn't blame him. Sadie's thirst for sex was unquenchable, though he'd known that when he'd fallen for her.

They never spoke of their arrangement with me but it wasn't difficult to figure out what made him the most comfortable. And I was *not it*.

Pushing those thoughts away for the time being, I focused on the way she used to look at me. With lust and complete abandon. Those sultry green eyes so clearly focused on mine. Running my hands over her soft skin, I lost myself in her again, in them and the rapture of our melding bodies.

"Now," I moaned when I was ready and Ryder pushed all the way in, rocking with me as I rocked down on Sadie.

"Oh fuck yes," she wailed, pushing herself into me, thrusting with us.

Ryder exploded first, pumping hard against me and crying out. I ground my hips up and down, fucking Sadie with the other side of the dildo and grinding against her clit. As she bucked and cried out I knew she was close, and I leaned down to bite her tender neck.

"Yes, oh yes," she screamed as I sank my fangs into her and slammed her over the edge. Her blood tasted like honeysuckle and I lost myself, drinking her down. I didn't need to drink, I'd had one of my donors recently, but Sadie tasted so damn good. And the hormones my bite released would send her flying.

Her peak lasted minutes as her entire body shook beneath me and I could hold back no longer. Raising my body up, I rode her orgasm into my own as it ripped through my body like a tornado, rushing headlong, devouring everything in its path.

Chapter Six

Waking up in bed sandwiched between the two of them was my idea of an almost perfect Sunday morning. If only Jared were there too.

Sadie rolled over and threw her arm around me, pulling me close. "What a wonderful distraction," she purred in my ear. "Coffee?"

"Yes, please," Ryder said from the other side of her. And to think I used to be the center of a Sadie sandwich. *Suspiro.*

Sadie got up, gloriously naked. Her curly red hair flowed over her shoulders and down her pale back, stopping right above the porcelain orbs of her pert buttocks. I was happy she'd been letting her hair grow.

"So what happened last night?" Ryder asked once she'd left the room.

"What do you mean?" I asked, feigning innocence.

"Come on, Burg, we both know that you can and do take sexual conquests home from the V on a regular basis. I don't think you've ever called us at two a.m. for a booty call."

"This new girl . . . and guy," I shook my head and rolled onto my back, "they got me all hot."

"And bothered, apparently," Ryder teased. "So why didn't you bring them home or take 'em at the club? Is the girl straight?"

"No idea. They're new to the Edge and I couldn't get a read on them."

"That doesn't seem like you. Why didn't you just ask?"

"The girl's going to be dancing there and I didn't want her to feel uncomfortable in case it's just my own desire and not hers. She's really shy."

"Who's really shy?" Sadie carried a tray with three cups. She handed Ryder and me coffee and took her own cup of tea off the tray before setting it on the nightstand.

"Burgundy met some new potentials last night."

Sadie lay down next to me on the bed. "Oh, do tell."

I blew on my coffee, cupping it between my hands. "Nothing to tell. Yet."

"Well," Sadie snuggled into me, "when there is, I'd better be the first to know."

"The second." I kissed the top of her head.

We spent another hour in bed but I was the third wheel, watching while they fooled around. I liked spending time with them but I didn't want to encroach on their space. They were kind to put up with me since I was . . . Well, number one, I was Sadie's oldest lover. Number two, I was funding her business. And number three, I was her best friend. But their cocoon was impenetrable, and they always made it clear that everyone in their bed was nothing more than a guest star. *Otro suspiro.*

"Thanks, unicorn," said Sadie in a giggle when I left, letting me know exactly where I stood in their relationship, yet oblivious to my angst.

As I was driving home, my phone buzzed and I threw on my headset to answer. *"Hola, mi padre, como estas?"*

"I'm returning your call, baby girl." My dad's gravelly voice sounded like he'd been smoking a cigar.

"There's an opportunity here for work."

"You mean my baby girl's finally going to go legit?"

"Not for me, Pop, for you." I told him about the

position the Council was gunning for. "It'd be perfect for you."

"That sounds great but Margery is finishing up a big case here."

"Can you come without her and then when she's done she can join you?" There was silence on the other end of the phone. "Papa?"

"It's not a bad idea. I'll run it by her. She can't stand to be without me though."

"Can't fault her for that." I smiled. "What's her case anyway?"

"The divorce of a very famous television actress. She often handles celebrity divorces."

I'd forgotten she was a divorce attorney. Would a celebrity-courting barracuda support his underdog fights? "Hey, can I give Benedict your number and he can call you directly?"

"Sure, sure. I have to go now, Deenie needs me."

"Te amo, Papa." But he'd already hung up.

Grumbling to myself, I reached for my Bluetooth when my phone vibrated again. I was going to ignore it, but Tiyah's name flashed on the screen.

"Hi!" I answered.

"Is now a good time?" she asked.

"Wouldn't have answered if it wasn't."

"Can you meet?"

"Sure, where?"

"I feel funny asking this but can I come to your

house? I really need a sympathetic ear and don't want to talk in public."

I wanted to fist-pump the air, but I refrained. "Of course," I replied calmly. "Give me thirty minutes though, I'm heading home now." I gave her my address.

I spent most of the allotted time changing into one of my tighter-fitting lace dresses, with my cleavage on prominent display. Thankfully, my room-mates were all out when the doorbell rang.

"Wow," Tiyah said when I opened the front door.

I wasn't sure if she was referring to me or Rex. The mammoth creature sat like a statue at my side.

"You look amazing." Her eyes roamed over me and I smiled.

"As do you." She was fitted entirely in black leather. I almost lost my shit right there at the threshold. She wore a short skirt and bustier so tight they looked painted on. I half expected to see tendrils of smoke rising from her. Her hair was now free of its earlier plaits and hanging down far past her shoulders, straight and black. "Please, come in." I motioned her into the living room, gesturing to the couch.

"What a gorgeous house." Her head swiveled, taking it in.

"Thank you. Tea?"

"Please."

I retreated into the kitchen, returning a moment later with a tray, two cups and a teapot, which I placed on the living-room table. I poured us both a cup and sat next to her.

She rubbed her hands on her pants and looked up at me, licking her bottom lip. "Okay, well, this is a little embarrassing but here goes."

I took a sip of tea, moving my cup to my lap and resting it there.

"Elijah. He's so great. And everything in our relationship is wonderful. The way he treats me. How attracted to him I am. He's attentive, not overly controlling, a complete gentleman. He has a great job, plans for the future . . ." She stopped and took a sip from her cup and then met my eyes. "There's just one thing. And it's so small I thought I could overlook it but . . ."

"But?"

"I can't seem to get it out of my head and I thought maybe you would have some insight."

"Maybe. What is it?"

"I have these fantasies." She looked away and down at the floor, taking a deep breath and holding it.

"Go on. Please. I may be the least judgmental person around." I smiled, placing my cup back on the table as she lifted her eyes back to me.

"I figured," she said. "So I've never been in any type of relationship other than your standard one."

"Standard?"

"I've never experimented."

"With?"

"Anything."

"And you want to?"

She looked at Rex, who was lying on the floor. "I want to be dominated," she said quickly, keeping her gaze averted.

"Oh." I wriggled on the couch. "And?"

"I've spoken to Elijah about it. He's not opposed to it but he doesn't know what to do. He's never tried anything like that before."

"Are you asking for my help?"

"I-I've heard that you—" Warmth flooded her dark cheeks. "At the club, someone was talking about how you . . ."

"Topped them?"

She nodded.

"And you want me to teach Elijah how to top you?"

She placed her own teacup on the table, sinking back into the couch and covering her face with her hands. "Do you even do things like that?" she spoke between her fingers.

"Can I train a Dom? Is that what you're asking?"

"Yes."

Gently, I tugged her hands away from her face. "I can and I do. I'd love to help." I gave her a full smile, teeth and all. "There's no need to be embarrassed about your needs, your desires. They're natural."

"Oh thank you!" She threw her arms around me and squeezed.

I squeezed back. The mere act of touching her dampened my panties. Perhaps the training would lead to more with this woman. Shit, just seeing her tied up, vulnerable and naked was enough. Almost. Burying my mouth in her hair, I stifled a snort. God, I was acting like Rex being offered a bone-not a good look for a Domme. Could watching me with his girl and teaching him how to top her encourage Elijah to want more? I certainly hoped so.

"When do you want to start?" My face was still buried in her hair, those pheromones jumbling my thoughts.

"As soon as possible."

"Great, let's figure out a night to start. You talk to your man and text me with some ideas. I'd like to do it at the club, if that's okay with you."

"In one of the back rooms?"

"Exactly. They're all set up for play, and it's a little more official there." And keeping things businesslike would remind me that, at this point, they only wanted me for my expertise, not for sex. Would seeing them together hurt, watching yet another couple play happy-happy? Not if I was in charge.

She nodded, pulling away. "That would be great, just great."

"And Elijah? He wants this too, yes?"

"Very much. He's willing to do whatever it takes to make me happy."

Lucky girl.

Chapter Seven

A few days later, Jared, Chrys and I were cleaning the house for my father's arrival.

"Where's he staying?" Jared was polishing the coffee table.

"At Inn Above the Ocean."

"Oh," said Chrys, "that place is pricey. No?"

"Burg's dad is filthy rich," said Jared. "He bought her this—"

"That'll do," I interrupted.

"He's coming here first?" Jared changed the subject.

"Said he'll check into the hotel and then stop by. He's never seen the house." This worried me a little since he *had* paid for it, which is why we were cleaning up so well. I wanted to make him proud.

The doorbell rang and Rex ran over, barking.

"Oh shit, he's early." I smoothed the front of my housedress, a lovely black velvet number that was tame for me, and went to answer. "Rex, stand down." The Rotty sat, watching the door with a look that said *I'm here if you need me.*

Opening the door, I was immediately struck with how different my father looked. He'd lost a lot of weight and was darker. Tanned. When he smiled, those teeth almost blinded me. Bleached? I threw my arms around him and he body-hugged me back awkwardly.

"You look well," he said through a clenched jaw as I held the door open for him.

"And you." I smiled up at him. "Welcome to Casa Mañana. This is Rex, our dog. You remember Jared? And this is our newest roommate, Chrys."

My father completely ignored Rex, who tried to push his wet nose into his palm. He held his hand out to Jared instead, who shook it, and then he hugged Chrys, as was our custom. "Sadie moved out? Or is she hiding somewhere?" My father looked around the living room.

"She moved in with her fiancé, remember? I told you months ago."

"Yes," he waved his hand about, "I forgot."

Rex whined and my father's eyes narrowed. "Why on earth would you get a dog?"

"He was a gift from Sadie and he's great protection."

"You can protect yourself," my father scoffed.

"Trackers came here and vandalized the house," Chrys said.

"Oh yes." My father looked around again. "I remember you saying that. Tour?"

Double take. "Of course." I waved him toward the kitchen.

After taking him through the house, I ended with the yard. "And here's our outdoor relaxation spot," I said with a flourish, opening the back door.

He stepped outside, eyeing Jared's landing pad. "You have a permit for this?"

I nodded. "Of course."

"Good." He put his hands on his hips and walked back inside. "I can't say that we have the same taste in decor but it suits you, *mi chica*." He leaned in and kissed each cheek. "I'm going to rest at the hotel for a while but I forgot to ask. Do you have an available donor? I'd like to replenish after such a long flight."

Vampires in the same family didn't usually share their donors. It was very personal—for me especially, since I had sex with all four of mine as well. "I can ask," I hedged.

"Be a doll and have one sent over to the Inn." He patted my cheek.

"I'll see what I can do."

His eyes flashed. "You'll see? No. No, sweet Maria. You'll do. And . . . make it a beautiful woman. I'm sure you have at least one female."

"Of course. I'll send someone as soon as I can."

"Thank you, love." He offered me one of his enigmatic smiles and headed out, calling over his shoulder, "Nice to meet you, Chrys."

After the door clicked shut, Chrys appeared at my elbow. "He didn't say goodbye to Jared?"

"Must have been an oversight," I said. But my father was calculating. He rarely did anything without a reason.

Chrys meandered toward the couch, plopped down and picked up her Kindle, leaving me to dwell. The decor I'd painstakingly chosen for my house suddenly appeared garish and bright. Is this how it had looked to my father, decorated by an eccentric teenager who'd just moved away from home? All it needed was a Starry Night poster, and it would look like every college dorm room in America. I winced.

"I'll be back in a few minutes." I fled into my bedroom, then stopped in front of my full-length mirror. Studying my reflection, I took several deep breaths, lingering too long before I reached for my phone.

"Burgundy," Amber drawled upon answering. "I didn't expect to hear from you for another week."

"I have a favor to ask, Am. My father is in town

visiting and would feel more comfortable drinking from one of my donors, rather than going to a vectum."

"Oh . . . of course. That's different, but your family is my family. Shall I pop over?"

"Would you mind going to his hotel?"

"Normally I'd say no, but for you, anything. It would be an honor to service your father. I can tell him what a wonderful job he did by bringing you into this world." She giggled.

"Thank you."

"I may ask for an extra orgasm next time I see you," she said with a smile in her voice.

"I may give you three."

After giving Amber my father's location and details, I texted him to tell him she was on her way.

I hope she is up to my standards, he texted back.

My father had always been partial to gorgeous female donors. Oh—had Margery started as one? It wasn't uncommon for vampires to fall for their donors, I supposed. My mother had always been jealous of my father's interests, but I'd told her that drinking from a beautiful woman was not the same as cheating. They'd been monogamous though, as far as I knew, and married for a very long time, almost a century.

My mother and I had a difficult relationship at times. It'd always been that way. Being a "daddy's girl" probably didn't help matters, but she always seemed weak to me and I had a hard time respecting that. Weak and insecure, even crying and carrying on when my father left to meet a beautiful female donor or colleague. If she'd truly suspected him of cheating, why had she stayed with him?

Personally, I couldn't imagine being with the same person for a month, let alone a century. Though I did believe in polyamory for myself, I also firmly believed that all parties should be informed and in agreement. There's no integrity in philandering.

Chrys handed me a cup of tea when I returned to the kitchen.

"Everything okay?" Jared looked up from a book.

"I think so." I took the cup, nodding my thanks, and sat next to him at the kitchen table, relaying my dad's request.

"I know it's not typical, but I can imagine it from his point of view. He's in a new area, he doesn't know or trust the random donors that show up at the banks, but he trusts his daughter's."

"But isn't he rich enough to go to a high-end vectum where all the donors are thoroughly screened?" asked Chrys.

"Maybe he likes the idea of sharing something this intimate with his daughter," suggested Jared.

I got up to pour more hot water into my cup. "I

normally hate having rules about everything but I wish there was one for this."

"Weren't they trying to get something like that passed a few years ago?" Chrys met me at the kettle to refill her own cup.

"Yeah. Actually, my father was one of the lawyers who fought it."

"And won, apparently." She raised her eyebrows.

"I think the idea of letting the final decision remain with the donors themselves was best for all," said Jared.

"One would think," I said, "but oftentimes they choose to become donors because they don't have other options for earning or because they're addicts trying to support an addiction."

Chrys gasped, bringing the kettle to Jared and refilling his cup. "I thought they screened for that."

"At most vectums, yes, but at some of the more budget levels, they let anyone in."

"Makes sense," said Jared. "It's not like drugs or alcohol in their systems affects you."

Sometimes I wished it would. I only drank alcohol for the taste, but most vampires didn't drink or eat anything at all. That I could not imagine; food was delicious and worth every extra pound. And it would be nice to be able to check out of my feelings the way humans and other Signum could with a little imbibing.

"So which one of your donors are you sending to your dad anyway?" asked Chrys.

"Amber."

"Whoa." Chrys sat down at the table, placing her cup down on the polished wood with a thud.

I looked over at her questioningly.

She turned a pretty shade of pink. "I'd be so jealous if Carter were to drink from a woman that gorgeous."

"You'd be jealous if he drank from any woman," Jared scoffed. "Who do you think you're fooling?"

The pink flush of her face went crimson. "Okay," she held her hands up, "you got me."

"Isn't Amber trans?" asked Jared.

I shrugged. "Yeah, so?"

Chrys looked between us, her head swiveling. "I didn't know that," she exclaimed.

"No reason for you to." I gave Jared my stink eye. "Why'd you even bring it up?"

"I know how old-fashioned your father is, is all. I wondered if he knew or if you were going to tell him."

"There's no reason to tell him that." I was getting annoyed. "It's no one's business. He asked for a donor, that's all. Who cares if she's trans?"

"No. No. You're right." Jared sighed. "I just thought that if your dad were to find out, he might be freaked or pissed."

"I don't think he'd care, and again, it's a moot point. He's not fucking her."

Sharing a donor with my dad was certainly pushing boundaries, but sharing sex partners was akin to incest. My stomach roiled at the thought of it. And why the hell would Jared even insinuate that?

Chapter Eight

Since Jared, Alec and I didn't have to work that night, we all went to Promise, the local ecstatic dance club at the foot of the pier.

As usual, the boardwalk itself bopped with teens and young adults, being a safe hangout for the under-thirty crowd. Unfortunately, the circus tent, its flags flapping in the fall breeze, would close soon for the winter months.

Inside, Promise was at least ten degrees warmer than outside, with sweating bodies bouncing to frenetic beats. The club drew the yoga and spiritual crowd since it was based on a specific five-rhythm dance foundation. The DJ spun all forms of techno, ramping up at the beginning of the night with slow beats that peaked fast and furious before dropping back down and ending in low-tempo jam. Most patrons wore flowing pants and skirts with cotton tanks. Some went topless but since it was an all-ages club that didn't serve alcohol, those were usually just the men. The few young kids that attended were in a separate room with a trained sitter who helped them with art projects. The around-eighteen crowd was often lying on a rug at the far end, zoning out on the ceiling light show.

I was moving to the up-tempo beats with Jared behind me and Alec in front. Being a Burgundy sandwich had its advantages, even though I knew that unless both of them were ridiculously drunk, nothing would happen. My eyes were closed when the body behind me disappeared for a second and then was replaced by small, pert breasts rubbing my back. I reached my hands behind and grabbed the woman's waist to pull her closer, leaning my head back to catch her scent. Strawberries. It was Amber.

Spinning around, I took her mouth in mine, sucking on her plump lips. She moaned and ground her body into mine. "Well, isn't this a surprise," I broke the kiss to whisper in her ear. "We're not due for a session until next week."

"I needed to see you," she said.

Pulling back, I captured her gaze. "Is everything okay?"

She bit her bottom lip, smearing the beautiful shade of coral.

"Let's go sit for a minute." I pulled her off to one side where thick exercise mats were spread out for people to relax on and watch the lights or other dancers.

She lay down completely on her back and I couldn't help but straddle her, pushing my groin down into hers. Amber was all woman but had decided to wait on her sex reassignment surgery and she had the most delicious "shenis" I'd ever seen. Immediately I knew something was wrong when she remained soft.

"Tell me." I looked into her eyes. They were a honeyed brown with shades of green and even turquoise.

"Shit, Burgundy." She looked away. "I think your father made a pass at me."

"Hey." I gently touched the side of her jaw, stroking her soft skin. "Whatever happened, it's not your fault."

I wished I were more surprised but first of all, who could blame him? Amber was stunning. And second of all, like father, like daughter. I *was* pissed though. It's one thing to think it and quite another to act on it, especially when you're putting up a monogamous front.

"Do you want to tell me what happened?"

"Nothing happened really, but while he was

drinking from me, his hands started wandering over my body."

I relaxed a little. "Maybe it was involuntary."

"Yeah? I wasn't sure. You're the only patron I've ever had and I wasn't sure if maybe sometimes that can happen . . . involuntarily, like you said."

I had heard it was more difficult for young male vampires to control their sexual urges while feeding and I didn't doubt it. But my father, at his age, shouldn't have that problem. "I'll talk to him."

"Oh no, please don't. I'd be so embarrassed."

"Well, if it made you uncomfortable, please don't service him again. I'll make some excuse for you."

She bit the inside of her cheek, her eyebrows drawing together. "He paid me really well and I'm saving money for my SRS. It's crazy expensive. I'd rather have him as a patron than not. I mean, while he's here. If it's okay with you."

"Whatever you want, sweetie." I leaned down to kiss her again and pushed my breasts into hers, moving my hand down to palm her groin. She moaned into me again and this time her anatomy responded pleasantly. I wanted to take her right there, but we weren't supposed to be overt with our sexual engagements at Promise. "Come home with me," I growled.

"I'd love to," she panted back, "if you're not otherwise engaged."

I grabbed her hand and forced it down my panties so she could feel how engaged I was. *With her.*

She put her fingers into her mouth, tasting me, those hungry eyes begging for more.

"Meet me at the exit. I'm going to tell Jared and Alec that we'll meet them at home." I rose slowly and helped her up, patting her butt as she went to fetch her purse.

The boys were grinding on the dance floor and I stood back to watch them first, enjoying the view.

"Hi," a soft voice said into my ear, and I spun around, almost knocking Tiyah over. Grabbing her shoulders, I steadied her, not wanting to know what would have happened without my vampire reflexes.

"Hi." I grinned at her. She looked even better than I remembered. I wanted to eat her right there. "What are you doing here?"

She looked away, bashfully biting her lip. "You mentioned the Wednesday-night DJ."

That's right. "You like?"

"Very much." Her lips curved, then flattened. "Are you leaving?" She looked disappointed.

"Yeah." I waved toward the door. "I'm meeting with a donor."

Tiyah looked down at her feet, which were clad in sparkly silver sandals with spaghetti straps, sexy as hell. "I'm embarrassed to ask but . . ." She trailed off, keeping her eyes trained on her feet.

"Ask away." I couldn't stop myself from touching her chin and bringing her head up, forcing her to meet my eyes. She let me. That look. Wham.

"I was just wondering if you maybe had a donor waiting list we could get on?" Her dark skin flushed a berry red.

Letting go of her chin, I held her gaze with mine, clearing my throat. I had people waiting, yes, but I did not keep a *written* waiting list. My donors rarely left me. A few had moved away over the years, replacing themselves with friends. Anyone asking this question was usually a vampire junkie or V obsessed. And the last thing I wanted was to pollinate that kind of fascination, but with Tiyah, I *wanted* her. No denying that. Maybe she was asking me because she wanted me too and couldn't think of another, better way to have me.

"No. No waiting list, but I'm full up on donors right now." I gauged her reaction.

Her ears pinkened slightly. "I'm sorry, that was rude of me."

"I have room for friendship, Tiyah." I reached for her hand and she let me hold it. "And more." I let the last two words hang in the air, watching her squirm, but she did not pull her hand away. Her grip actually tightened.

"There you are, darling." Elijah stood next to us.

He was speaking to her but he was looking at our hands. She immediately let go, turning to him.

"Yes, sorry, honey. I saw Burgundy and wanted to say hi."

"And I don't blame you one bit." He turned to me. "Good evening, Burgundy." His eyes traveled over my body, slowly. "Don't you look beautiful tonight."

"Thank you, Elijah. Nice to see you as well. I was just heading out."

"Oh." His voice lilted down. Disappointment. "Can we steal you for one dance before you go?"

"No, but—" I glanced at Amber, who was chatting with another woman while she waited for me. When she looked up, I held up a finger and shrugged. She nodded. "Elijah, I'd like to talk to you alone, please."

He followed after me to a far corner where I sat down on the carpeted stage.

"Tiyah tells me that you'd like me to teach you how to top her." I gauged his reaction.

"That would be great." He leaned forward eagerly. "I should have asked you myself but I didn't realize it was so important to her and I don't know what the protocol is."

"No, that's fine, but I need to hear it from you and discuss some things."

"All ears." He threw me a wolfish grin.

"Do you want me to top her while you watch, or

do you want me to tell you what to do as you top her?"

He shook his head, gaze resting on a corner of the ceiling past my head. "What do you usually do in these situations?"

"I usually top the person with their partner watching so they can see how it's done and mimic it later. But I've also been hired to teach the partner to top them. It's a matter of preference. The downside to that is we don't remain in the scene. It's more instructional and can come across like I'm topping you, topping them, which can be a turn-off for some subs. In that case, what I usually suggest is that I train their partner to top someone else first."

"I don't want to do this for anyone else." Elijah met my eye. "I'm only doing it because it's what Tiyah wants and I want to please her."

Uh-oh. Did he perceive himself forced into this situation, or was he excited by the possibilities? "You'd prefer to watch while I take the reins?"

"I would." The man wore a gleam, the pale blue of his eyes brightening for an instant.

Playing the exhibitionist, especially with these two, was a turn-on if all parties were on board. My heart rate increased at the thought but in matters like these, it was important to remain professional.

"And how much in that realm are you comfortable

with? This is where we negotiate things like intimacy and the acts of bondage themselves."

"Intimacy? You mean you'd have sex with her?"

"I will only do what you're comfortable with. It can be purely bondage and discipline without sex. And in that realm we negotiate how much discipline and what kinds. That we negotiate with Tiyah as well. The submissive is the one with the control. She decides how much or little she wants and it's our job to listen and push her to those limits." Outside of the BDSM community, most people had this idea backward, that the Master or Mistress was in control. But this work wasn't about being controlling or mean, it was about listening to your partner's needs and meeting them, but also knowing that sometimes they really needed to go just a *little* bit farther.

Elijah nodded. "I like the sound of that."

"And then there's the intimacy part. Some people like it when the Domme kisses, touches or even has sex with their partner during the scene, but I will not do that if you and Tiyah don't want me to."

"What do you usually do?"

"Usually," I gestured with my hands, "sex is involved, but not always. I've had people come to me for just humiliation or discipline. It depends on a person's kink."

He shrugged. "I don't know what her kinks are."

"Why don't you talk to her in private and find

out? We can negotiate further later, but now I have another commitment. Have fun dancing!" I threw them my smile and headed out to Amber, who was waiting like a saint for me by the door.

"My house?" I asked.

"Please," she moaned. "I want you to make love to me."

Chapter Nine

My night with Amber had been divine, even though it'd seemed like I had to steer my thoughts away from the couple every few minutes. Still, I managed to give my donor just what she needed and stay present with her. *Enough*.

Margery and her daughter, Deenie, were supposed to arrive over the weekend and I'd asked my dad for some father-daughter quality time before they did. I fully expected to have plenty of alone time with him after they came to the Edge, but I also wanted to respect the time he needed to put into his budding relationship.

I met him at the Inn on the pretense that we'd look at houses together. He wanted to rent something before they arrived so that everyone wouldn't have to live in a hotel. A real estate agent I was not, but I'd found listings for a couple of open houses high in the hills that had views overlooking the ocean, which is what he'd asked for.

"I don't know why you insist on driving this old Camaro," he said as I drove down Discovery Highway, the main drag that led from one end of town to the other.

"Are you kidding? I love Cherry. She's solid and beautiful."

"Just like you, kiddo." He smiled over at me. "You get that from your mother."

"Dad, what happened between you and Mom?"

He sighed and started cleaning his fingernails. "We grew apart. It happens. I'm a businessman, you know that. My work has always played a big role in my life, and your mom, she doesn't have any business aspirations."

That was harsh.

"It wasn't until I met Margery that I realized what was missing in my life. Sometimes they say that you have to find something you love to know it's what you've wanted all along."

"But you and Mom seemed so happy."

"A cada pajarillo agrada su nidillo."

People like what's familiar.

"We were never truly happy. We tolerated each other, we were comfortable with each other, but we weren't happy. And yet until I met Margery, I didn't know that. *A la ocasión la pintan calva.*"

Opportunity knocks only once.

"So . . . where did you meet?" I was afraid to ask and afraid not to.

"At the courthouse. She was trying a case right after me and my case was running late. The judge called for another recess, and though it wasn't my job to tell her, I did."

"That was nice of you."

He gave me a sheepish grin. "You know I've always been a *ventosa* for a pretty woman."

"Like father, like daughter." I laughed and he stiffened.

"That's one of the many things I'd like to talk to you about." His dark eyes flitted to the window.

"What?" He refused to make eye contact with me.

"Well, Margery and her daughter are a little more conservative."

"Conservative? How?" I turned up a steep hill that would take us to our first destination.

"They're not prejudiced, it's just that they aren't quite used to, well, your type of lifestyle."

"What does that mean?"

He turned toward me. "Come on, Maria, you know what I'm trying to say. Just tone it down until they get to know you better and are more comfortable here. Okay?"

"Dad," I bristled, "I'm not comfortable with that."

"I'm not really asking you, Maria. I'm telling you."

I pulled over outside the open house. "And if I refuse?"

He leaned toward me and put his hand on the back of my neck, squeezing. Hard. "Don't you and your friends just love your house?"

My breath caught. He wouldn't dare. Would he? An old memory came flooding back. He'd bought me my first car in Nicaragua, but when I'd introduced him to my first girlfriend, he'd immediately taken it away. "Are you saying you'd sell my house?"

"Sell it? No, Maria." He let go of my shoulder. "I would never do that to you."

I relaxed.

"I may need to ask for your help with paying the monthly mortgage though."

What? He'd told me he'd bought the house outright. "Very funny, Dad." I pointed toward the house. "Let's go look at this one."

"Yes, let's." His voice was tight. He opened his car door and got out.

I followed him to the front door, walking a few paces behind. My mother had told me that my fond memories of him and our father-daughter bonding experiences were skewed, but I'd dismissed it. She'd always been jealous of our close relationship. And how would she know anyway? She hadn't even been there for most of them.

Sure, he could be an ass at times, everyone could. But my dad had always put me first in his life. And yet, another memory rushed in. I was eleven and had just fought with my mom. We stood in the living room, his hands on my shoulders. *"Maria, you must know that I will always love your mother more than I will love you. She comes first in my life and you will never replace her in my heart."*

I squeezed my eyes shut to block out the memory, almost doubling over at the long-forgotten sensation of being stabbed in the gut with his sharp words. He'd said what he thought would stop me raging at my mother, as preteens are wont to do. Every word he ever uttered was calculated to achieve his desired result. Completely normal behavior for a star attorney, and understandable. I certainly hadn't made it easy for anyone to parent me, growing up.

A text pinged and I dug my phone out of my purse, but my father reached for my hand, turning to beam at me as he opened the front door. The house was lovely with dark wood paneling and wood-veneer floors. We were greeted by the sales agent.

"Welcome, Mr.—?"

"Rosales." He let go of my hand to shake hers and then added his other hand to cover it. Her perfectly coiffed blond hair gleamed in the track lighting above, and her soft skin turned a pretty shade of pink as he held onto her hand for just a beat too long.

"And this is—?" She looked at me.

I opened my mouth to speak but he cut me off. "My wife, Maria."

"Oh." She looked as shocked as I probably did.

"No, no," he laughed, "I am making a joke." He waved in my direction. "This is my mistress. My wife, she arrives tomorrow." He winked at her.

"Dad," I admonished and he guffawed loudly, raising his eyebrows at the agent.

Awkward.

"We wish to look at the house now," he said, pushing past her. The poor woman stood perfectly still, her eyes wide.

"He's quite the joker," I said to her.

"I see," she responded stiffly, not bothering to follow.

I caught up to him in the kitchen. "Hey, Dad, that kind of skeeved me out."

He flicked his wrist at me dismissively. "You never could take a joke."

That wasn't true.

"This kitchen is awful," he said to the agent when she entered, still looking flustered.

"It could use some upgrades, yes," she agreed, regaining her composure. "But it has lovely bones."

"Awful," he grumbled, walking around it. "Margery

will hate it." He turned to me. "If it's not modern with granite or marble countertops and brushed-stainless-steel appliances and fixtures, we will have to tear out everything and replace it all."

How did he know the woman's tastes so well after only a few months? "Surely she's not that inflexible," I said.

He looked down his nose at me. "She has impeccable taste, there's a difference. It's one of the many things I love about her. She knows what she wants and will not settle for anything less. Unlike your poor mother."

Ah yes, my mother the people pleaser. A timid little mouse, always afraid to stand up for herself. Of course a woman who knew herself and had strong opinions would please my father. Even challenge him. And an updated kitchen *would* be prettier.

"Do you want to look at the rest of the house?" I asked.

"No. I don't mind paying for some upgrades but this would take too long." He waved his hand around. "The entire kitchen would have to go. Not to mention that wood paneling in the other room."

Dad had always loved wood paneling. What had changed? Maybe I was the one stuck in the past.

"I'd rather find something closer to our tastes. Margery won't want to wait for construction before moving in. Remodeling always takes longer than planned."

Couldn't argue with that.

"Meet me in the car," Dad said to me, turning to the agent.

In the car, I checked the text. It was the list Tiyah had come up with. Reading it turned me on, a lot. She was up for quite a bit. Hot! And her safe word was *tap* which was Jamaican for stop. And if that was too short she'd say *tap duh dat*, which meant "stop that." Good.

Dad hurried out of the house and back into my car right after I'd confirmed receiving their text.

"Let's hope the next place you picked has an updated kitchen," he said brusquely.

"Sorry, Dad, I hadn't realized that was an important feature." I drove further up into the hills, telling myself that my father's new taste was refreshing.

"Thank you for sending me Amber, by the way." He smiled from the passenger seat. "She's one hell of a looker."

"She is, yes."

"Are you—? Have you," his smile twitched up even more in the corners, "tasted that?"

"I would rather not answer that particular question."

His teeth shone in the morning sun. "You just did."

What the hell had gotten into him? I knew he liked beautiful women but he'd never acted this inappropriately before. Had he? I shrugged it off. He was just being silly.

He stared out of the window. "Great views of the ocean up here."

I agreed, parking in front of the next place I'd marked. "I hope you like this one, it has those great views."

He appraised the house before walking toward the front door. "Very modern. I like it better already."

"Since when do you prefer modern architecture over rustic?"

He didn't respond.

Chapter Ten

The next morning I showed up at the courthouse in the center of town for a private, three-person meeting. Benedict was currently in charge of the Council but that title rotated yearly. Walking into the circular lobby, I was still unclear as to why he had asked me there. I wasn't on the Council, so I couldn't sit in on their nonpublic meetings.

"Burgundy." My vampire boss appeared at my side like the eye of a storm.

"Yes, sir."

He cupped my elbow, manhandling me to the side of the room. I let him. "Your father's waiting for us inside the Council chamber but I wanted to talk to you first."

I cocked my head the way Rex did when I asked him a question.

"I know that you have some influence over your father's . . . decisions."

"Well." I steepled my fingers in front of my chest, hoping to appear more in charge than I really was.

"There's a very sensitive matter at hand and your father doesn't exactly see things in the same vein as I do."

"Did you want a yes-man or someone more opinionated who might challenge you? Because if you wanted the former, my father is not that man."

"I'm hesitant to discuss more before you hear what's on the table. Can you remain after to speak privately if need be?"

"Of course." I followed him to the ground-floor meeting room.

My father was seated when we entered and I pecked him on the cheek.

"Dad."

"Mari— Burgundy." He adjusted his tie without making eye contact with me.

We sat across from him.

"The reason we needed a Signum lawyer on the Council," Benedict said to me, "is because there are some specific laws we want to change and we need to make sure everything we're doing is legal."

"Okay," I said. "And?"

"And I don't agree with the changes they're proposing," my father snapped.

"Are they illegal?" I asked.

"No," he responded stiffly, "they're too lenient. Distant Edge is a refuge for our kind." He spread out his arms. "And to open up our borders to include . . ."

"Werewolves," finished Benedict.

"Them," sneered my father. "It's not safe."

I leaned on the table. "Werewolves? I thought they were a myth."

"Well, they aren't," said Benedict, his tone even and calm.

"So there's another breed of Signum?" I asked.

"They're *not* Signum." My father's voice dripped with condescension. "They're barely more than animals."

"Then what are we? Or shifters?"

"Shifters can control their changing," my father returned, pointedly ignoring my first question. "They cannot."

"Have they been in hiding all these years?"

"Yes." Benedict turned to me. "I know what an advocate you are for Signum rights, and since your father is specifically a Signum-rights lawyer, I asked him to sit on the Council in order to help with the influx of weres."

"If those creatures move here, I'm leaving. And I'm taking my family with me, including you." He looked at me pointedly. "No one else will be comfortable living with them among us either. Are you prepared to lose half the population here?"

"Why should they be considered any different than we are?" I matched Benedict's tone, low and composed. "They're Signum too."

"Wild beasts are what they are. Uncontrollable. Feral," growled my father, pounding his hands on the table.

"Dad," I kept my voice calm and rational, "why don't we give them a chance? You of all people should understand the prejudice and fear they're trying to overcome. It wasn't that long ago when you fought the humans of Granada to carve out a home for our people and our family."

"Enough." My father stood up, then rounded on Benedict. "Is this why you had me come here? To turn my own daughter against me? Make her fight your battle?" He turned to me. "I thought you were better than this, Maria. And I thought you cared more about your little house." He stormed out into the lobby without a backward glance.

Benedict pushed his chair back, and I followed suit. "I'm sorry for assuming your father would listen to you and putting you in the middle of that."

"You knew I'd be pro-werewolf even without knowing they previously existed?"

"Of course. I know you. I know how much you care about everyone, humans included."

Apparently he knew me better than my own father did, and that stung. "Now what?"

"Now the Council votes."

"Right now?"

Benedict nodded. "If you're interested in the outcome, you can wait in the lobby." He stood and went to open the door for the crowd of Council members who stood outside, waiting to come in.

Among the twelve who entered was a tall, good-looking guy with slicked-back blond hair and a three-piece suit. I didn't recognize him.

"Who's that?"

"A new Council member," he whispered. "He replaced Adam, who moved to Sedona last month for his wife."

Ah yes, Adam was a shifter, so this new guy must be one too. In order to maintain balance, three of each race of Signum and three humans sat on the Council. That way no one could strong-arm another race. My father brushed past me with what sounded like a growl. He had replaced one of the vampires who had moved out of the country with his family.

"Burg, I'm sure I don't have to tell you that this topic is currently under wraps?" my boss said.

I forced myself to nod, teeth clenched.

"Good." He jutted his chin and I left to wait in the lobby.

Chapter Eleven

"Are you working tonight?" Jared asked when I got home.

If I hadn't been sworn to secrecy, I would have shared the shocking news with my closest friends. Not only was there a whole new race of Signum, but the Edge was full of cowardly bigots. Well, the second part wouldn't have surprised them. And it wasn't *full* of bigots. The vote had been a tie, six to six.

"Yeah. Why?"

"So's Alec. I thought I'd come watch you both dance and hang out."

"And if I weren't?"

"I'd take you to the movies or something." He walked over and put his arms around my waist. "I can tell you had a bad day."

"I'm exhausted. My dad . . ."

"What'd he do this time?"

"Nothing, Jared, he didn't *do* anything." I bristled. Why didn't he understand that my dad was a hard-ass because he wanted the best for me and the Edge?

"Did he find a house to rent?"

"After hours of looking, yeah, there was one that finally passed muster."

"I didn't know he was so picky." Jared let go of me, sitting on the couch.

"I don't think it's him. He kept saying, 'Margery only likes modern,' and 'Margery only likes brushed steel.' " I collapsed on the couch next to him and he pulled me in.

"I'm sorry, Burg."

"I'm sure she's great. I guess they're just still in that new phase of their relationship when they're so concerned with being perfect for each other." She must be amazing for Dad to be so enamored with her, and I was happy for him. He must have stayed with Mom for so long because he felt obligated, and that was no way to live.

"Are you guys having a cuddle puddle without me?" Alec walked into the living room and flung himself on top of us.

"Never." Jared threw his arms around his man.

My phone beeped.

"Who's that?" asked Jared.

"Geez, doesn't she get any privacy?" said Alec.

"We tell each other everything," said Jared.

"Everything?" Alec raised his brows.

"Yes, darling, everything." Jared looked over my shoulder, reading the text.

It was from Tiyah. I bit back a sigh. That woman and her husband were dreamy. Dreamy? Really, Burg? I sounded like a damn teenager, but I hadn't been this excited about anyone since . . . ever. *Snap out of it. It's just infatuation.*

Jared pecked my cheek, still staring at my phone screen. "Ohhh, that sounds promising."

"Dammit, you two. Now I want to know." Alec tried to look at the phone too.

"It's the new woman who was hired at the V. I'm showing her around tonight, after my set."

"Showing her around your titties," laughed Jared.

"Whatever." I got up and went to shower.

The Club was always hopping on the weekend, and that night it was in full swing. I had gone in early. Tiyah had wanted to meet up before her set and I was helping her get ready in the main dressing room. She perched on a stool in front of the bank of mirrors, applying her makeup.

"You're going to be great," I said encouragingly.

"I don't know, I've never stripped before. I'm classically trained."

"Don't think of it as stripping. I don't. It's dancing. It takes a lot of skill."

"Can you go on with me?" She looked like she was about to cry.

"Benedict's never promoted a doubles act here."

She stood up. "I'm going to go ask him."

"Wait."

She stopped.

"You're serious?"

She nodded. "I can't do it alone. I don't really need this job. Elijah makes enough to support us both."

How? As a dive instructor? "Hell, no. You wait here. I'll talk to the boss."

Benedict's office was upstairs where he could survey his kingdom. I knocked on the door.

"Enter."

He was sitting behind a bay of monitors, watching the scenes below. There were cameras everywhere, even in the sex rooms, but Benedict didn't have monitors for those rooms. Tapes would be watched only if someone got hurt.

Swiveling around, he eyed me quizzically. His gaze trailed down and then back up, which surprised me. For years, Dr. Benedict Volkamoff had given off the distinct impression that he was asexual, ever since moving here from England and purchasing the V. Either the man's libido had just woken up or he'd accidentally let his guard down.

"Dr. Volkamoff."

"Ms. Rosales." He smiled. "You must want something."

"Yes, sir, it's the new girl."

"You want the new girl?"

"Most definitely, sir." I grinned back. "But I would not come to you about that."

"I would hope not." He swiveled his chair back toward the monitors.

"Tiyah's not used to the kind of dancing we do here, and though I know we've never done couples acts, I was hoping we could, just for her first dance. So I can help her out."

"I did not hire Ms. Clarke for her shyness."

Shit. Not good. "Yes, sir. I'll go tell her." I turned to leave. Should I ply her with drink?

"Wait."

I stopped with my hand on the doorknob.

"I trust you, Burgundy. Do it and let's see how it works." He tapped the monitor trained on the stage. "I'll be watching."

"Yes, sir. Thank you, sir."

Benedict liked things to be his idea; simple, really.

Back in Tiyah's dressing room, I helped her pick out an outfit that would match mine: two black sequined numbers like something out of Cabaret.

I picked music from the soundtrack and spent twenty minutes teaching her some moves and sketching out some choreography for the set. She was a fast learner.

We appeared on the darkened stage together, striking a pose with me behind her, as the lights rose to illuminate us. The clapping began in earnest.

Throwing some of the choreography to the wind, I leaned toward her ear, breathing deeply. Sandalwood and peaches. Did she taste like peaches too? Focus.

"Let's go off cue a little. Follow my lead, okay?"

Her head nodded against me.

Dropping my hands to her waist, I held her there, following those gyrating hips, matching her movements with mine. I let my hands flow up and down her sides, reaching in front of her to slowly unbutton the pinup dress she'd settled on. Her back arched, revealing her white lace bra as it peeked through the top of the dress. She pushed her ass back, grinding it hard against my crotch. Ignition.

Turning my head, I spied Elijah moving toward us through the swaying crowd, his gaze pinned. On me? The bulge in his pants was evident even from this far away. Still, his lips were tight, and his eyes were narrowed, almost at half-mast. Either he was out of his mind with lust or he was at war with himself over an unwanted attraction. I lowered my lids and licked my full bottom lip. He sucked in one of his own in response, chewing on it while his gaze clung to me like a rock climber about to lose his foothold.

Tiyah moved my hands up to cover her bra, shimmying and grinding into me. While I unhooked the front clasp, she continued unbuttoning her dress, letting it drop to the floor. I circled to her front, offering my hand to help her step out of the fabric pooled at her feet. In turn she busied herself with my outfit, slowly running her warm hands over my form. This was, by far, the hottest dance I'd ever put on at the V, and my G-string was drenched to prove it.

The dance lasted until we struck our last pose fifteen minutes later, both of us breathless and wearing nothing but pasties and G-strings. We were supposed to be looking at the audience, but instead, we gazed at each other.

"Fantastic job," I whispered at her when the lights had lowered again.

The crowd flew out of their seats, clapping and yelling—the first time since Alec had come to the V.

"Bravo!" "Encore!" "Why haven't they had doubles acts before? That was brilliant."

I reached for her hand and she took it. I led her

backstage where Elijah stood, arms folded tightly over his chest.

"Oh baby. Wow." He threw his arms around her, smiling over at me as he clung to her. "Very sexy. Burgundy, you two were amazing together."

Chapter Twelve

Benedict approached us at the bar where the three of us sat in a row. "Your act together worked surprisingly well. I'd like to see more. Can you develop at least one more to roll out by the end of the week?"

"Tiyah?" I asked.

"That would be great." She clapped her hands together. "I'm much more comfortable dancing with Burgundy."

"And you two looked amazing together," said Elijah.

"Good, then it's decided. We'll announce it in tomorrow's newsletter." Benedict turned and walked away.

Tiyah excitedly touched my arm, and whether she did it on purpose or not, I didn't know, but her breast rubbed against me, shooting a jolt of pleasure straight to my crotch.

I glanced at her man and he was smiling and nodding. "I can't deny that it turns me on to no end, watching you two together." He licked his lips.

I would have to work to compartmentalize because I wanted nothing more at that moment than to kiss her.

A throat cleared behind me and I turned to see my father standing with a woman I didn't recognize.

She was surprisingly short, not quite five feet, with straight, stark-white hair styled into a long bob. Her face was an unlined oval. The eyes peering at me looked almost feline except they glowed aquamarine. She had to be wearing contacts. The woman was very pretty, though I hadn't expected anything less. Dad had standards and if he was leaving Mom, I had no doubt he'd traded up. But still, her severity surprised me. In the past he'd liked softer, more feminine styles.

I leapt off my stool to throw my arms around him but he only briefly hugged me back, stiffly, before pushing me away.

"Maria, I wanted to introduce you to Margery and her daughter, Deenie." He motioned toward a girl who appeared to be in her late twenties or early thirties, the spitting image of her mother with the same white hair. Deenie wore hers long down her back, almost to her waist. Neither woman was looking at me; their heads were craned toward the stage, watching Alec, mouths unhinged.

I placed my hand on his shoulder and leaned into his ear, "Dad, why did you bring them here?"

"You told me this is where you danced and it was a club for vampires. You did not tell me you were a stripper." His eyes flashed.

It was true, I hadn't actually told my parents I was stripping but more out of respect for their ages than out of fear of judgment. I shrugged. "It's not like anyone gets completely naked here. It's just fun."

"I don't even know what to say right now, Maria. This is not a place for ladies. Margery and Deenie are ladies," he said loudly.

And I wasn't? His remark certainly chafed but surely he hadn't intended it to. Was he just trying to keep peace with his new woman?

"Now, now, Hervé." Margery turned toward him and linked her arm with his. "We're here to meet your lovely daughter. Let's not make a bad first impression."

There we go. But at the same moment, her body language belied her words. Those eyes sizing me up were cold. Calculating. Was I misreading her? Being thrown into a new and different element, especially this one, could make anyone uncomfortable.

"Maria," she extended a hand toward me, "your

father has told us much about you." She looked me up and down, her eyes trailing slowly from my face down to my silver stilettos and then back up again, pausing at my waist and cleavage. "He did not, however, mention what a big girl you are. My, my." She flashed her teeth. "It must take a lot of work to," she waved her hand over me, "look like that."

Deenie covered her mouth with her hand, stifling either a laugh or embarrassment, I couldn't tell which.

Immediately my attention swung to my father but he was smiling at his lady and absently caressing her back.

"Excuse me?" I said to Margery.

"Such a lovely girl." She smiled at my father. "Your wife did such an . . . interesting job with her, don't you think?"

My father either had no idea this woman was putting me down or didn't care. I chose to believe it was the former. "*Si, si.*" He smiled at her. "Burgundy was a handful. As you can tell, she always had her own mind." He narrowed his eyes at me.

Reminding me that he'd asked me to rein it in for them?

"Mama, can we leave?" Deenie's high voice hung in the air. "I don't like it here. I thought we were going to a classy place."

"Darling," she purred at my father, "will you take

Deenie and wait for me outside? Please?" She blinked her thick, mascara-clad lashes at him and Dad nodded quickly, escorting Deenie out by her elbow without saying goodbye to me.

"Let's talk a minute, shall we, dear?" Margery nodded at the far end of the bar.

"You can talk to me right here."

"I love how spirited you are." She leaned in closer. "I make your father very happy, and I know you love him and only wants what's best for him, yes?"

"Of course."

"Well then, you can play by my rules and be welcomed into our family with open arms, or . . ." She leaned back, crossing her arms over her chest.

"Or?"

"Well, let's just say I wouldn't want to think of the alternatives."

"Are you threatening me?"

"Oh my, no. I would never." She moved her hand to her chest and held it there. "We both want what's best for your father, I know we can agree on that."

She sneered, her lips stretching over her top and bottom teeth, wide and gruesome.

"I hope you'll come to"—she air quoted—" 'dinner' at our new house tomorrow night."

I shook my head. "Why would I do that?"

"So we can get to know each other better, plus,"

she looked toward the door to the club, "your dad has some exciting news he wants to tell you."

Without waiting for a response, she turned and left.

"What the hell was that?" Jared asked, leaning over the bar. Tiyah and Elijah looked between us, not speaking.

"That's my dad's new girlfriend. I really hope I just caught her at a bad time."

"Or maybe it won't last?" said Elijah.

"One can hope," I agreed.

"Why'd your dad bring her here?" asked Jared.

"No idea."

Chapter Thirteen

I'd been lost in thought after meeting my dad's new squeeze. I wanted so much to please him. Surely I could give this woman and her daughter a chance.

Dad had picked Mom, after all. And though she'd always been kind to me, I'd never truly respected her for not pursuing her own dreams and always letting him push her around. She had to put up with his moods, she'd told me once, because he supported her financially. I'd vowed never to put myself in a position like that. Maybe this new woman was good for him. She'd keep him in line. Challenge him.

"Hey, gorgeous. You're thinking too much," Elijah said into my ear.

"Sorry." I waved my hand around my face. "Wanna take my mind off of it?"

"We're ready when you are," he said and Tiyah leaned over to smile at me.

A good scene was always the perfect distraction. "Meet me in the blue room in seven minutes."

"Which one's that?" asked Tiyah.

"You'll figure it out." I threw the rest of my drink back and left the bar.

Seven minutes later on the nose, they entered the room with wide eyes, their heads swiveling like tops. I stood at the foot of the bed, gauging their reactions, waiting and imagining it all from their perspectives. A brushed-steel bed frame was pushed against the wall opposite the door, leather cuffs on all four corners. The mattress was permanently covered in black vinyl and bare. The side tables contained antiseptic spray and cloths to wipe it all down, as well as a jar of condoms and other assorted disposable options. At the foot of the bed I'd placed my small trunk of travel implements. And of course there was the cross.

"Oh wow," said Tiyah.

"Changing your mind?" Elijah asked.

"Not at all." She set her jaw and proceeded forward.

"Stop." I said and she did, looking between me and her husband.

"Stand here and do not move from that spot.

Elijah and I have some things to discuss." I walked out of the room with the man trailing me.

In the hallway I leaned close to him. "I want to make sure you're okay with all of this. I know she is."

"More than okay." His voice caught, but he looked down at his own crotch. Anyone looking could see he was telling the truth, physically. But emotionally, I wasn't so sure.

"Nice package you're sporting there."

He beamed, then bit his bottom lip, looking worried.

"Elijah, it's okay if you don't want to go through with this."

"No, no, I do. I'll do anything to make her happy."

"What about your happiness?"

"Look, Burgundy," he met my eyes, "it's important to me that I try. Maybe I'll hate it and then we'll deal with that. But maybe I'll love it too. Doing things for your partner is part of a good marriage."

That's why Dad was asking me to tone it down for Margery. I pushed the unwelcome thought away. "Okay, I'm going to take the lead, obviously. But I will ask you to do certain things so you can get a feel for it all. And if anything makes you uncomfortable . . ."

"Yes?"

"Let's come up with a safe word for you too."

He nodded. "Banana." He raised his eyebrows and looked down at the one between his legs.

Stifling a snort, I walked back into the room with him trailing behind me. Tiyah had not moved. Good girl.

"Strip for us," I told her.

Elijah licked his lips. I pointed to a metal chair and he took a seat.

She started pulling at her clothes, but I held a hand up. "Stop."

She did.

"Slowly, like we practiced." My voice was soft and encouraging.

She nodded and began to gyrate her hips, running her hands up and down her body.

"Touch your tits," I commanded and she immediately cupped her lovely breasts through her suede bodice, pushing them up so the edges of her dark areolas appeared. "Pinch your nipples. Tease them so we can see."

Between her thumb and forefinger, she rolled her nipples out, twisting them to attention. I wanted to see how hard she played with herself so I would know how hard to push her. The pinching was rough and she quickly grew flushed, her lids dropping, her breath coming faster.

"Pull your tits out of your top."

She pulled out one and then the other so they

spilled over the edge of her tight bustier. Elijah groaned as he rubbed himself over his jeans, his eyes flitting to mine. I gave him a curt nod.

"Pinch one of your nipples and pull up your skirt so we can see your pussy." My breath hitched as she lifted the hem slowly, exposing the closely shaved crop of dark hair below, not even long enough to curl. I wanted to see more.

"Spread your lips open and touch yourself there."

Complying, she brought her other hand down, took a wider stance and spread open her gorgeous lips. It was difficult not to drop to my knees in front of her for a taste, the dark pink flesh beckoning like a beacon. We both watched as she circled her clit and then pinched it as she had her nipples. Good.

"Rub yourself."

Tiyah complied with my demands and I resisted the urge to touch myself. Barely.

"Strip everything off," I growled, "and get on all fours on the bed with your ass in the air."

She looked surprised as she quickly removed her clothing and climbed onto the bed. If only I could stop the clock to admire her beauty. I'd seen her strip before, but the parts that had been covered before stood at attention now. Dark, pert nipples and the smallest patch of closely cropped dark hair. Her husband watched me watching her, his eyes glittering in the soft light, imagining what his stunning bride looked like through my eyes, no doubt.

I tore my gaze from her to pull my riding crop from my trunk. It was the easiest implement for newbies to use and I motioned for Elijah to join me. We stood behind her as I showed him how to spank, encouraging him to mimic my movements with an open palm.

We didn't speak so as not to break the scene.

Slap.

I gently rubbed Tiyah's smarting skin, then pointed at him to do the same. We took turns smacking and stroking her luscious ass until she was warmed up. I curved my hand under to feel her pussy. It was warm, wet and throbbing. I grabbed Elijah's hand and put it between her legs so he could see how turned on she was. Then I motioned for him to stick two fingers inside of her. When he started to pump her canal, I slapped her ass with the riding crop. She bucked forward and yelped but I pulled her back by her hip.

"Don't move. Call out your safe word if it's too much, okay?"

"Yes." Her voice was low and garbled.

I removed Elijah's fingers and put them in my mouth to suck, tasting her for the first time and almost passing out at how utterly delicious she was. So sweet. He groaned, pushing his fingers in deeper. I bit him and he yanked his hand out quickly to my disapproving head shake.

Tiyah looked behind her and I whacked her ass again, hard. Harder than I had before. She cried out and faced forward, lowering her head.

"Good girl," I cooed, running the riding crop between her butt cheeks and down, further, against her swollen clit. She wriggled her ass against it and I removed it to hit her again, then rubbed the welt that was forming.

"Get up," I said and she did, moving her hand to rub her ass.

The St. Andrew's cross stood upright, mounted to the wall. "Go to the cross and press your back against it." When she'd situated herself, I showed her husband how to secure the buckles around her wrists and ankles. Then I had him stand aside to watch as I ran my hands up her body, lightly tickling her heated skin. She watched through heavy lids, licking her lips, her eyes darting between us. I grabbed her tits and squeezed, sucking on a nipple and pulling it into my mouth.

Elijah watched us intently, his eyes swiveling between us like he was taking mental notes. But he was also biting his lip again.

I jerked my head in invitation. I didn't want to speak and break the scene.

He came close again and ran his hands greedily

over her body, staring up into those magnificent eyes. I slapped her inner thigh, one eye on her reaction and another on his, and then motioned for him to take over.

When she yelped, he stopped abruptly and I shook my head at him. I showed him how to alternately slap her tits, rub her heated flesh and then bite and pinch her nipples. As he grew more confident, I slapped and he rubbed before we alternated. His hits were far too tame. Grabbing a blindfold from my trunk of tricks, I fastened it around her eyes, then whispered directions to him.

Within minutes, she was writhing and he was performing like a pro, but that look of utter concentration and worry still creased his face. So I took one of his hands and placed it between his wife's legs with my own. She was drenched even more and I trained my gaze on his, watching his eyes widen before he buried his face there, wrapping his hands around her hips, breathing her in.

She moaned, jutting her hips forward, and I placed a hand on his shoulder. He looked up at me with a glassy, half-lidded smile and I crouched beside him.

"Can I eat her or do you want to?" I whispered.

Elijah looked up at her face, then back at me, his eyes lingering on my lips before he nodded. Letting go of her he pointed at me and stood.

"I'm gonna lick your woman's clit now," I enunciated for her sake.

"Yes, please," he rasped.

I dropped to my knees, taking her. Sweet. She tasted the same way she smelled, like sunshine and just-plucked peaches ripe from the tree.

Tiyah moaned, pitching forward. Luckily, the straps held her up as her knees buckled. There was no doubt that I was an expert at cunnilingus. I was probably spoiling her.

Pressing my face into her groin, I breathed in her warm scent again, flicking my tongue lightly over her bud.

"Harder," she cried out and I stopped, picked up the riding crop and swatted her inner thigh. "Ouch."

I ran my hands up and down the tender flesh, following with nips from my sharp fangs. Chancing a look at Elijah, he had one hand on her slight frame and the other rubbing himself, watching me intently.

"Elijah, grab a dildo but first cover it with a condom," I commanded, running my tongue up her crease. A moment later, I held out a palm and he complied, placing one of my larger dildos on it, wearing its raincoat.

Tiyah's mouth widened, those lovely lips plumping under her tongue.

"Are you ready for penetration?" I asked her.

"Yes," she rasped.

I ran the dildo hypnotically over her body, zigzagging from one breast to the other, across her stomach and down to her heat. Playing with her clit with one hand, I plunged the vinyl cock into her.

"Yes," she cried as I pumped and played.

I motioned for Elijah to crouch next to me. "If you want to pull out your cock and join in the fun," I licked my lips, "I'd like that."

His eyes darted back up to his wife's face and then back to me. Head bouncing on his muscular shoulders, the low light cast his blond curls in dark shadow. Eagerly he pulled out his cock, commanding my stare. It was magnificent. Thick and long. I had to bite my lip to refrain from falling on it but my eyes met his lidded ones. He looked between my lips and his cock but we hadn't agreed on that with Tiyah. I gave him a quick shake of my head, shooting my glance back up to her face, and then returned my focus to her pleasure.

He stood up and pressed his hardness against her, running his hands over her body and practicing his open-hand slaps. Every time he hit her she moaned, urging him on. I alternated pumping her with the fuck toy and licking her, bringing her right to the edge before stopping.

"Please," she begged.

"If you don't shut the fuck up, I'm going to gag you too. Understood?"

"Yes." Her voice was barely audible.

"Yes what?"

"Yes, Mistress."

"Good girl. Elijah, your turn." I motioned for him and he crouched next to me again, putting his hand on top of mine. His hard cock hit my leg and he leaned forward as though he was going to kiss me but I shook my head. I wanted to grab him but refrained, moving back to the toy chest for my flogger.

While he sucked, licked, fingered and pumped her, I ran the thin leather fringe over her body, pausing to take her mouth and squeeze her nipples.

Her breath came quicker, shallower. She was close.

"Stop fucking her," I called to him and he did.

She whimpered but, as instructed, she didn't say a word.

I whipped her tits with the flogger, expertly crossing one side of her body and then the other as Elijah watched, his cock in his hand.

"I want you to come all over her," I said to him and kept whipping her while he squeezed and pumped himself.

"I want to watch. I want to see you two together," she groaned.

"Shush," I slapped her face, hard, but I pulled off her blindfold.

Biting her lip as those deep eyes held mine, she mouthed, "Sorry, Mistress".

Sucking her mouth into mine, I whipped her harder as she thrashed in pleasure. When I pulled away, her eyes were locked on her lover's cock. He was close, standing wider, head back, breaths shallow.

When he spurted over her stomach, she bucked and strained, opening and closing her mouth as though trying to taste him.

"Now we make her come," I said and he dropped back down to fuck her hard with the dildo, licking and sucking.

I cupped her tits again, pinching the nipples between my fingers and rolling them, then tugging. Her eyes widened, her breathing rapid, her body rigid. I covered her mouth with mine, tangling our tongues and sucking on hers, pinching those hard nipples.

It took only seconds to make her come this way with both of us pleasing her, and when she did, her entire body rocked and undulated. Her scream rang through my mouth as she shivered, pitching and moaning with the orgasm. I broke the kiss and Elijah held her thighs open so we could both watch her waves of ecstasy.

"Taste her come," he whispered to me, "it's divine." I needed no more encouragement and latched on, drinking down her nectar. He was right, the woman was the most delicious thing I'd ever tasted.

Her orgasm was long as I teased out wave after wave with my own mouth, and when she was spent, she sagged on the cross, her lids closed. I jutted my chin toward her ankles and began unbuckling her wrists but her eyes flew open.

"No, not yet," she said.

"What?" She needed aftercare.

"I love being tied up like this, and I want Elijah to make you come while I watch."

We exchanged glances and he nodded at me.

I was wound up tight, having soaked myself over the exchange. I strolled over to the bed and lay down, facing her, and spread my legs so she could watch while her man pleased another woman.

Chapter Fourteen

Back at the bar, sipping my last nightcap of the evening, I was successfully avoiding Jared's incessant questioning.

"A lady never eats and tells," I admonished after his third ask.

"Really? Since when?"

"Don't you have drinks to serve?" I cradled my own in my hands, lazily spinning around to see who was on stage. But there at the end of the bar was Elijah, without his woman. He looked distraught, his head resting in his hands on the bar top.

I made my way over to him, touching him lightly on his shoulder. He jerked up. His eyes were bloodshot like he'd been crying.

"What's wrong?" A sudden surge of protectiveness

washed over me. "Do I need to punch someone for you?"

He managed a wan smile, shaking his head.

"Did you and Tiyah have a fight?"

"Something like that," he admitted.

"Jealousy issues?" In my experience, that's what happened when a couple brought a third into their bedroom. Fantasy was always better than reality.

He eyed me warily, then took a swig of his drink. "Sit down." He motioned to the stool next to him and I took it, leaning close enough for the alcohol on his breath to burn my eyes. "I'm so conflicted."

"About?"

"That was just about the hottest thing that's ever happened to me. During the . . . *scene*, I was loving it. I even entertained thoughts about doing it again and again."

I leaned closer, placing a hand on his shoulder. "But?"

"I'm a man, Burgundy. It's my job to protect my woman, not beat her up and whore her out." He brought his glass up, tilting his head back to down the last of it in a considerable gulp.

"Hey," I rubbed his upper back, "I know this is difficult, and if you can't do it or don't want to, you don't have to. But here's my 'but.' " I flashed my fangs when he glanced at my face. "Your woman wants this; she's the one who asked for it. So that makes you a proper Dom, a proper alpha male, to be man enough to deliver."

He clenched his jaw, the muscle pulsing as he hailed Jared for a refill.

"I encourage you to talk to your wife about this."

"I tried. She got pissed and went home. She told me to find another place to sleep tonight."

Oh crap. "I do not want to come between you two and I don't want to give you the wrong advice."

"I thought I knew her so fucking well. I thought she was happy with our relationship, with what we have. And now suddenly it's not enough. *I'm* not enough."

How I could relate to that. Too well. That's how I felt whenever I was with my father, especially now that his new woman seemed to pull his strings. But had I ever truly been enough, even before Margery?

And what about Jared and Sadie? I wasn't enough for them either. Jared, for sure, needed a man to fill his intimate desires but Alec filled his emotional ones now as well. Sadie had Ryder so she no longer needed me, emotionally or otherwise. No matter how much I tried, my friends left because whatever I gave them just wasn't enough.

Chapter Fifteen

Sitting in my dad's new living room the next afternoon, I waited patiently for the women to bustle back into the kitchen.

"Why did you bring them to the club last night?"

"They wanted to see where you worked. Something about meeting you on your own turf so you'd feel more comfortable," he said. "Had I known it was a strip club, I never would have brought them."

I rearranged myself on their new white leather couch, crossing and then recrossing my legs.

"And speaking of, Maria, I really wish you'd chosen to wear something a little more conservative tonight." He glanced toward the kitchen.

"Really, Dad? You want me to change who I am for your new girlfriend?"

"That's not what I meant and you know it. It's

respectful to meet others in their house in a way that will make them feel comfortable. Did your mother teach you nothing?"

Shit. He was right, I wasn't even making an effort. "I'm sorry, Dad. Do you want me to change?"

His features softened. "How about you button your jacket up?"

I complied, fastening the tiny red seed buttons on my Victorian-era red velvet jacket. He was doing me a favor, trying to make sure that Margery liked me.

Deenie entered, motioning to the dining room table. "Dinner's ready."

I cocked my head at my father. He gave a little shake of his head. I had assumed they were vampires too. Apparently I was wrong.

"Thank you so much for accommodating my schedule." I sat down next to my father. "I have to work later."

"And by work, do you mean taking off all your clothes for leering men?" asked Deenie.

"Deenie, manners please," snapped Margery.

"But mom, you said—"

"Deenie. Hold your tongue. Now."

"Yes, Mother." She looked down at her plate.

Margery smiled. "I know most vampires don't eat, but apparently you're not like most vampires, now are you, dear?" She winked at me. "I made pasta primavera, sautéed brussels sprouts and mashed potatoes." She waved her hand across the food steaming at the center of the table. "Please, help yourself."

I sat on my hands for a beat. Were her back-handed compliments unconscious? Everyone waited, all eyes on me.

"It smells delicious," I said.

Margery let out a sigh. "Thank you, I've only recently started cooking again."

"What did you do before? I take it you're not vampires?"

"We're witches," said Deenie proudly.

Crap. That wasn't good.

"We've always had a servant," replied Margery. "And we'll get one here too, won't we darling?" She eyed my father.

"Yes, sweetheart, of course we will."

"Why?" I genuinely wanted to know.

"Mom doesn't like to cook," said Deenie. "Plus she has more important matters to attend to."

"Why not cast a cooking spell?" I asked. "And cleaning spells?"

Margery visibly stiffened. "Our magic isn't quite that strong. We're from a lesser line. I grew up with servants; it's what I'm used to."

"I see." Why did I think she was lying? What reason would she have?

My father helped himself to some of the pasta

and I stared at him openly. I'd never known my father to eat food before.

Margery tapped the side of her water glass and we all turned to look at her. "I have an announcement to make."

My eyes darted left and right. Dad did not seem perturbed in the slightest. Actually, his chest was puffed out a bit. I grabbed the sides of my chair as though I were on a roller-coaster ride.

Margery lifted her left hand and wiggled it in front of her face, giggling like a teenager in heat. Was that a wedding band?

"Oh, Mama," Deenie squealed, practically knocking her chair over to stand and hug the woman. Well at least I wasn't the only one who didn't know.

I looked at my dad, a smile spread wide across his face, fangs protruding. But why? Why would he do this?

"Are you even divorced from Mom yet?" I couldn't help asking.

"Of course he's divorced from your mother," Margery scoffed. "We would not have legally been able to get married if he wasn't."

"Well," I said stiffly, "congratulations."

"Thank you." Margery beamed. "You can refer me to me as your wicked stepmother." She cackled. The woman actually cackled.

Dad laughed. "You're such a card."

Sometimes he couldn't hide his ripe old age of ninety-nine. I briefly wondered how old Margery was, younger than Dad or Mom, no doubt. But the less magic a witch possessed, the more quickly she aged. It was why Aurelia didn't look a day over forty, yet she was actually 187. The Holts were the strongest witch family in the world.

I took a bite of the food, drowning myself in potatoes and pasta. Surprisingly, it was quite good. At least the woman could cook. Not that Dad had any use for that. "Delicious food, Margery," I said.

"Why thank you, Maria."

"My name is Burgundy." It was out before I could stop it.

Father tsked me. "Maria is the name we gave you."

"Burgundy is the name I've been using for the past twenty years. If you refer to me as Maria in public, no one will know who you're talking about."

"I like the name Burgundy." Deenie blinked her sky-blue eyes at me.

"Thanks, Deenie. So where are you two from? You don't look Nicaraguan."

"Maria, manners," my father snapped.

"No, no, Hervé," said Margery. "It's a fair question." She turned to me. "We're transplants from Spain."

"My father was Swedish," said Deenie.

I knew I should have asked how they ended up in

Nicaragua, but I didn't really care and continued eating in silence. I gobbled up the meal far too fast.

"Well, I'd love to stay longer," I pushed my chair away from the table, "but I forgot that I promised someone a ride into work and I have to leave. Thank you for the lovely dinner."

My father stood up abruptly, following me to the foyer. "When did you become so rude?"

"When you married another woman without telling your family first."

"Maria . . ." He reached for my hands. "It was unplanned. Margery's idea. As soon as the divorce from your mother was finalized she," he glanced toward the dining room, "she couldn't wait."

Margery appeared in the foyer, smiling. "That's right, Burgundy. I couldn't wait to sink my claws into him. He is quite the catch."

My father laughed boisterously. "Such a jokester she is."

She narrowed her eyes at me. "He really shouldn't have married a divorce lawyer. If he tries to leave me, I'll take him for everything he's got, and we both know he's got a lot."

My father laughed again. "Yes, she tells me I can't afford to divorce her."

"It's true, Hervé."

He hadn't insisted on a prenup?

"But why would I ever want to, darling?" He

moved to her, his arms circling her waist. "What's your other favorite saying?"

She preened. "Let's spend all the money so there's none left for the kids."

Both of them broke into peels of laughter. They didn't even notice me leave.

Chapter Sixteen

Sitting in my car, I had to take several deep breaths. Was she for real? Couldn't be. I sincerely hoped that was an act. I couldn't figure her out. Either she was one sick puppy or she had a cutting sense of humor. Neither option endeared her to me. But she made my father happy and we had a very special father-daughter bond. I'd put up with her, for him.

I looked at my phone, surprised to see several text messages from Elijah.

Hey, Burgundy, can we meet up with you later? We can't stop thinking about the other night.

That would take my mind off things. *Sure*, I pinged back. *Where and when?*

You tell us, we're open.

I started my car and headed home. If my father

and his new scary wife hadn't shown up at the V yesterday, I wouldn't have hesitated to tell them to meet me there, but it no longer felt safe. The sex rooms didn't have doors, and though I did not think my father or that witch would return there, I couldn't be sure.

Pulling into my carport, I sat still for a few minutes, thinking. Why would he marry that woman? There must be something I was missing. I grabbed my phone and dialed.

"*Hola, mama.*"

"Maria. *Como estas?* Is everything *bueno?*"

"I'm confused, Mom. Did you know that Dad remarried?"

A little sob escaped and then a sniffle. Thousands of miles away, and she sounded like she was in my living room. "*Si, chica,* your brother told me."

"That's crazy, right? How long has he known this woman?"

"For years, I think. I heard they were seeing each other while we were married."

I twisted a lock of hair between my fingers, shaking my head. I'd never thought of my dad as a cheater. An actual cheater. He had some double standards, culturally that was even understandable, but a cheater?

"He said her firm handled your divorce. Are you

sure she wasn't involved?" I didn't want to ask, but I had to.

"Not that I saw, but maybe behind the scenes. I'll never know."

Jesus. "What did you settle for?" I hadn't wanted to pry, but with that woman sinking her claws into his fortune, I had to ask.

"He didn't want the house or even partial custody of your brother, and he gave me a lot of money. Plus he's paying child support and alimony."

"So he just walked away from it all?"

"*Si.*"

Even if he had given her several million, he hadn't taken a hit, but it still didn't make sense.

"Mama, do you think that woman could have put a spell on him?"

"No, *chica*. Your papa was always mean spirited, you just never saw it."

She had always been jealous of our relationship, trying to cast doubt. Even now, she played the same games. "Why did you stay with him for eighty-four years then?"

Her sigh through the phone line tugged at my heart strings. "I've told you before, *chica*, I had no skills to make it on my own."

"He would have paid alimony and child support, that's no excuse."

"I didn't want to break up our family."

"So you suffered in silence, for your children?" What a martyr. Though how would I have reacted in the same situation? Growing up, I'd had a tumultuous relationship with my mother. She'd always acted jealous of me, even once intoning that my father pitted us against each another, but I'd never believed her.

"I have to go," I said. "Are you doing okay? Is Juan?"

"*Si*. We're better. Will you call me tomorrow?"

"*Si*, Mama. I love you." I hung up, more confused than I had been before calling.

My head hung low as I walked up the steps and through the gate. A cold wind blew through the front yard, swaying the cedar tree and running through the bare limbs of the Japanese maple.

As I walked in the house, I inhaled deeply, catching the scent of freshly baked bread. Ryder or Iphi must be over; they both loved to cook. Candles burned in the living room, casting shadows from my elaborate metal-and-tapestry boho shades. The sights and smells of home. My home. Maybe it was unconscious on their part, but the tone of the ambiance let me know that this was where I belonged. And that made it possible for me to discard all the earlier friction.

"Burg!" squealed Iphi, bounding from the kitchen to throw her arms around me.

"Iph." I smiled at her. "Pleasant surprise."

"Chrys wanted me to show her how to bake bread."

"Nice. Is she here?"

Iphi gestured toward the kitchen, where sounds of clanging emanated.

I looked around. "Where's Rex?"

"Jared and Alec took him on a walk." She eyed me sideways. "Is something wrong?"

"Yeah." I twisted a strand of hair. "But I don't wanna talk about it. I'm gonna go take a shower."

I left Iphi gaping after me. She was a sweet girl, the sweetest of all three sisters. But finally being at home, all I wanted to do was relax.

After turning the water as hot as I could handle, I shrugged out of my clothing and stood under the jet, soaking my skin. I squirted some shampoo into my hands, wet my mane and scrubbed.

There was a knock on the bathroom door and then it opened a crack. "Need some help?" Jared's voice cut through the steam.

"If you want," I grumbled, my eyes and mouth clogged with water.

He entered, closing the door behind him. I didn't look up. A few moments later the glass door to the shower squeaked as he stepped inside with me.

"Turn around," he ordered and I complied. An expert masseuse, he ran his long fingers through my thick locks, then scrubbed my scalp. The familiar tugs soothed my ragged nerves.

I groaned, my head tilting backward and then from side to side so he could get at all of it. "You're so damn good at this. Forget chiropractic school and become a head masseuse."

"Tell me what's going on. Let me in."

I shook my head but he held it still.

"I'll sic Rex on you if you don't."

"I'd like that."

"All right, I'm not going to push, but if you need me, I'm here."

"I know."

Jared finished washing and rinsing my hair and then helped me out of the shower and dried me off. I was torn between crawling into bed, pulling the covers over my head and blocking out the world or inviting Tiyah and Elijah over to play.

"Do you have to work tonight?" Jared asked.

Shit. "Yeah, I'm supposed to, but I'm beat." More like beaten up. Everything that had happened today had just been too much, as if a great tide had risen out of nowhere and swept me out to sea. I was tired of keeping afloat. I needed to rest for a while.

"Call in sick," he suggested. "I don't think you've ever done that before."

I hadn't. In all the years I'd worked at the V. "I can't, J, it's Saturday night. What will Benedict do?"

"Alec can cover for you and I'll text one of the on-call girls. I'll let Benedict know too."

An argument was budding on my tongue but my lids were growing heavy. *Tamp down those emotions, Burg.*

"Rest." He plucked my silk robe off the back of the door and wrapped it around me. With one arm around my shoulders, he escorted me to my room, laid me down in bed and pulled the covers over me.

"I don't want to . . ." I was saying when sleep took over, dancing with me like a lost lover on a long-deserted stretch of beach.

Chapter Seventeen

A dream about swimming in a blackened lagoon with massive rocks jutting out at odd angles turned sexual when a warm tongue lapped between my legs. I pushed my crotch into the disembodied softness, reaching for the back of the ghost-head. My hands met actual hair and my eyes fluttered open. If it was one of my endless lovers waking me up this way, I was more than fine with it.

Except it was Elijah's face that swam into view, propped on one elbow next to me in bed, watching.

"Hi." He smiled through heavy lids. "I hope you don't mind that Jared brought us home for you. We were worried when we didn't hear back."

Oops, I'd forgotten to return his text. Sure enough, Tiyah's dark hair was bobbing between my legs and the moans emanating from her mouth matched mine. "Yes," I cried out, pushing myself into her. "Use your fingers. Open me up and fuck me with your fingers." She did as she was told, inserting first one wet finger and then two, pumping them in and out of me, slowly curling them upward. "Elijah," I croaked.

He jumped to attention. "Yes, Mistress."

"Direct her. Own her," I hissed through clenched teeth.

Elijah moved toward his woman, telling her how to please me. "Lift up her ass and lick her there."

Tiyah complied, groaning while she did it.

"Fuck her with your finger and rub her clit," he commanded.

"Bureau, third drawer," I called out and Elijah moved with lightning speed, returning moments later.

He reached under Tiyah's long hair and grabbed it by the roots as I'd shown him, pulling her head up. The hungry look in her eyes told me he'd graduated to the next level. Topping her. He handed her something and whispered in her ear, then shoved her head back down, holding it there.

Something cold and hard entered my pussy. My metal dildo. I bore down but she teased the entrance as he growled instructions too soft for me to hear. I had a lot of experience training Dominants but it was always difficult for me to let go in this position, to be a bottom. Still, the most well-rounded Dom or Domme had to be a switch at times. Until we've experienced what our subs do, we cannot fully appreciate the trust they put in us and how significant it is for us to keep them safe. And how delicious it is to completely let go and push past our own limits. I willed myself to lie back and let Elijah lead.

"Good girl," he cooed. "Don't make her come yet. Bring her to the edge."

Tiyah pushed the metal inside of me and I bucked up into it.

"Lick her. Now," Elijah commanded and pushed her head down so hard that her teeth grazed me.

"Ouch," I cried out. It didn't really hurt. I was telling on her.

The sharp snap of a riding crop stinging her ass resounded through the room and she cried out, her nose and lips pressing into me.

"Bad girl," he said sternly. "Use your tongue on her, lightly."

Tiyah licked me while the sounds of a soft whipping filled my ears. "I'm punishing you for hurting her," he said. "Do you like it?"

"Mm-hmm," she moaned between licks.

"Your ass is so red," he said as he continued slapping it.

She spread me open with her hands and buried her face in my pussy, licking and moaning. The pleasure shot out from my clit through my extremities. No doubt I was dripping all over her face and the sheets as the sounds of her lapping filled the air.

I opened my eyes and propped myself up on my elbows to watch. Her ass was raised in the air, her knees resting on the edge of my bed. Elijah had gone from spanking her to licking her, bending over behind her, apparently tonguing her ass.

"Open your pussy up for me, Tiyah, I want to fist you," came his muffled voice. Her ass wiggled in the air as she spread her legs wider apart.

He moved off her to squirt some lube onto his hand and then made eye contact with me, biting his lip.

I nodded, bringing one of my hands up to show him the correct hand configuration. He copied me and I nodded again. She stopped licking to look up. I pointed to her and he grabbed her head and pushed it back down.

"Did I say you could stop?" he growled.

"No, Master," she said quietly, her breath tickling my cunt.

"Do what I said and bring her close to orgasm."

"Yes, Master." She went back to licking me and inserted the dildo again, pumping my hole.

I watched as he pressed his hand into her pussy, all the while looking between her backside and my eyes as I urged him on. She moaned and gurgled into me as his four fingers and thumb stretched her wider and wider. It might be all she could take and I held a palm up to him. He pumped his hand methodically in and out, maintaining the beak-like configuration. Tiyah pressed back against him, her body tensing and arching.

"Breathe," I commanded and she gasped for air, loosening her muscles just enough for his hand to slip all the way inside.

The woman shot up, crying out in pleasure. His hand was on her shoulder in a second, pushing her back on me, but the poor girl was lost in lust. I held a finger up to him and motioned for him to grab her by the throat. He did, holding her above me on all fours, her eyes squeezed tightly shut as I pantomimed to him to keep fisting her while I played with her ravishing chest, teasing and pinching her nipples for several minutes.

Sliding out from underneath her I reversed my body, moved back into position and placed my mouth over her slickened folds. My tongue found her clit and I latched on while she bucked and writhed, screaming loudly.

"Oh my god, oh my god, *oh my god.*" And she came all over us both, twisting and squirming, diving straight down to the warm depths of her own pleasure.

After her last convulsion we moved her back onto

the bed, working together, even though I could have easily lifted her with one hand. There, we held onto her until her breathing slowed, those lids sinking over her honey-colored eyes, those dark-pink lips curling into a smile. The three of us fell asleep, Tiyah spooning me and Elijah spooning her. Utter bliss. *Don't get used to it, Burg, these aren't yours to keep.* But I so wished they were.

I woke several house later to her tongue on me again and him standing over her, fisting his cock. "It's her job to please you," he said to me. "Let me make her do it properly."

"You'll have no argument from me, if—" I arched into her mouth.

His hungry eyes watched as his erection grew harder and harder in his hands.

"Anything," he groaned.

"You cover me with your come when I come in her mouth."

"Oh yes." His breath caught, then sped up. He cleared his throat. "You heard your Mistress, Tiyah. Make her come. Hard."

Chapter Eighteen

After spending most of Sunday in bed with the couple, I was confident that Elijah had all the skills he required to top his lady. I had successfully wrenched my thoughts away from the possibility of anything more than this experience. I was worthy of finding everything they had with someone of my own. What my dad had found with Margery. What my besties had with their mates. I wouldn't settle for less, even if the hole of solitude was massive, and growing by the second.

"Tiyah, can you wait in the living room while I talk to your man for a few minutes?" I asked and she dutifully dressed and left my room.

"How are you feeling?" I asked him.

"Really good," he said with a grin. "I don't know

how'll it be without you there to guide me but I'm willing to try."

"You can always call me after a scene. We can discuss it on the phone or meet for coffee. Whatever works."

"I feel like I should pay you for teaching me how to please my woman."

"I benefitted greatly, but if you'd like to pay me in diving lessons, I wouldn't say no."

"That'd be great. I didn't know you wanted to dive."

"Neither did I, but why not? It's something I've never tried and I'm always up for new things."

"Deal."

"Can you go get Tiyah so I can speak to her in private now?"

"Sure." He left my room, and a few minutes later there was a tentative knock.

"Come in," I called out, still perched on my bed.

She opened the door and I patted the space next to me. Sitting, she crossed her legs and rubbed her hands down the front of her jeans.

"I wanted to make sure that you're happy with the way Elijah is topping you. I'm ready to cut the cord and let you two move on to your D/s bliss."

She reached for my hand. I let her. "I don't know how we can ever thank you, and I know I shouldn't want this but . . ." she looked at me. "Can't we keep being intimate with you?"

I adjusted myself on my bed to face her. "That's not how these types of arrangements work. You two are basically monogamous, no?"

Nodding, she opened her mouth and then closed it again. "We have been but with you it's different. It feels right."

Fuck. It did feel right but that didn't mean it was. "Tiyah," I said softly and her eyes filled with tears as she looked down. I raised her chin up so I could look into those soulful orbs. "I'm not looking for a relationship with anyone. I love sleeping around and I need variety."

A tear rolled down her dark cheek, catching at the corner of her gorgeous full mouth. I used my thumb to stroke it away. A little sob escaped. "I think I'm falling for you."

"It's the oxytocin," I responded. "All those orgasms release the same hormone you feel when you're in love."

"That's not what this is," she insisted. "I know all about that hormone. It's the same one vampires can inject you with."

"One of them, yes."

"Look," she touched my hand again and stroked it, "I know what I'm feeling is real."

"What about Elijah?"

"Oh, I love him too. I want you both."

I stood up and walked over to my dresser, looking at her in the mirror. Watching her watch me. Shit. I wanted her too. And him. But that wouldn't end well. I had to take into account what had happened between Sadie, Jared and myself. And what would never happen between Sadie, Ryder and myself. In theory, triads were my number-one fantasy, but in reality, they were messy and unpredictable and imper- manent. These two had a solid monogamous relation- ship. The green-eyed monster did not look or feel good on me.

"I know Elijah is attached to you too," she said, her voice even.

"You've talked to him about it?"

"No, I don't have to. We've been together for long enough. I know."

"Tiyah," I turned around to face her, "what we had was amazing and I wouldn't change it for the world, but it's time for you two to explore a D/s rela- tionship on your own and see if it works between you."

"And if it doesn't?"

"If it doesn't, you'll have to figure out what does." Shit. They were under my skin, like a nail in one of Cherry's tires, and I would need something stronger than pliers to remove them.

Chapter Nineteen

So I did what I always did when I wanted to take my mind off things; I went to the V to have sex with a random stranger.

Jared wasn't working but I said hello to Carter briefly on my way to the back.

"Stay for one drink," he cajoled. "Please?"

"Bored?"

"With the conversation from this alluring crowd?" His sarcasm dripped down his freshly ironed button-up. "I'm that obvious?"

I barked out a laugh, clinking my glass of bourbon to his water.

A soft hand landed on my forearm and I reeled around, grabbing the person who touched me without my consent by the throat. Tiyah's lovely brown eyes bulged as I held her, dangling a foot off the ground. I quickly let go, catching her under the arms as she fell.

"Shit, Tiyah, I'm so sorry. It's a reflex."

"One she's honed for years," added Carter.

I shot him a look. Tiyah was shaking slightly, and in a minute, Elijah was at her side, his arm cradling her protectively.

"What happened?" he asked her, narrowing his eyes at me.

"Nothing," she coughed. "It was a misunderstanding."

"An accident," I said. "I apologize."

"Are you okay?" he asked her and she nodded, offering him a smile that lit up her face.

"I was so excited to see Burgundy here that I grabbed her without any warning."

I paused for a beat while he nodded, sighed and slipped onto the barstool next to the one I had vacated.

"I hope you two have a fantastic night." I turned.

"Wait," he called out.

Turning back to them, I rested my hands on my hips, tilting my head.

"Can I speak to you for just a few minutes?" asked Elijah.

"Of course." I remained standing.

"Tiyah, can I talk to Burgundy alone, please?"

"Oh," she looked between us, "yes. I'll wait, at one

of the tables on the floor." She wandered away, not looking back.

I resumed my perch, fingering my drink, not looking at him.

"I was hoping to see you here, to talk to you in person."

"Well, here I am."

"I'm not sure how to say this so I won't beat around the bush." He looked me straight in the eye. "I want a full-on threesome with you and Tiyah. I can't stop thinking about it. It's getting in the way of my relationship with her."

"Does she know?" I asked.

He nodded, then motioned to Carter. "Scotch on the rocks please."

"And what does she say?"

"She loves the idea." He looked at me again as Carter slid a drink down the bar.

"I'll tell you what I told your girlfriend. I don't do long-term. My four donors and my best friends are the only people I engage with sexually on a repeat basis, and even that I keep to a minimum."

"Why?"

"Simple. I like my lifestyle and I don't want to get attached. In my experience, relationships like the one you two have don't work out in the long run, and more importantly, I could never be monogamous."

His laugh was deep and not at all condescending

or minimizing. "Why not take a chance on us, Burgundy? We won't disappoint. We're not asking for your hand in marriage. Just a little more fun. It's obvious that you're still attracted to us."

"Attraction," I waved my hand in the air, "that comes and goes."

"What are you afraid of? You don't think that my wife and I are solid? Are you afraid of breaking us up?"

Like father, like daughter. I flinched. Except I wasn't a cheater. I kept my cards on the table in full view.

Maybe that was the problem. I wasn't very discreet. Hadn't I been asked nicely to play ball so I could keep my house? My life?

Or was it something else? It's true, they did seem solid as a couple. Shipshape and watertight, no room for anything to seep in between. The only thing worse than stealing one of them from the other would be to watch them both walk away.

I leaned toward him. "You two are great fun and great people, but I can't." They were a Band-Aid for my detachment. But I needed a tourniquet for these seeping emotions.

"Can't or won't?" he asked.

"What's the difference?" I shrugged. "Excuse me." I slipped off my barstool, making my way to the back rooms. The easiest way for me to reset my clock was to engage in some delicious depravity.

Chapter Twenty

I slipped through the beaded curtain at the entrance to the back rooms, then paused, running my hand down the ornamental charms. My palm wrapped around a string of sparkling glass beads, holding tightly. The way I wished someone would hold onto me.

The curtain was elaborate and sexy, like the couple I was trying to shed. Both were completely my style too. Large red beads mixed with silver, white and pale blue and tinkled joyously with every movement. The couple was forthright and accepting, pushing my emotional boundaries. Both were sensual. Provocative.

Snap out of it. Compartmentalize.

I peeked into the first room and was greeted with a voluptuous woman topping a man half her size.

Nice. She looked up at me, licking her lips, and motioned for me to enter. I shook my head. No bottoming for me. *Unless it was to help Elijah*, came the unbidden thought. No, not even then. That was over.

The second room sported two men. One was bent over and tied to a vaulting horse, while the other flogged him. I recognized the one on the rack: not bisexual.

The third room looked promising. A man I didn't recognize had another man that I did recognize tied to the metal chair. They both looked up and the one I knew licked his lips. Score. This one *was* bisexual and he liked it rough. I entered with a smile and joined the one I didn't know.

"Burgundy," I whispered into his ear. He pulled back and his gaze slid up and down, almost languidly, stopping at my chest.

"Oh I know exactly who you are," he grinned. "I'm Mark."

"Scott," I jutted my chin toward the one tied up, "an extra hand?"

"Oh please," Scott groaned. His cock looked painfully hard, probably due to the metal cock ring fitting snugly around it and his balls. His arms and legs were tied to the chair and Mark was holding a cane—just the way Scott liked it.

The last time we'd played, I'd opened bloody wounds on his ass as he'd cried for more.

His inner thighs and chest were welted, pre-come dripping from his raging hard-on.

Mark handed me the cane, then dropped to his knees to take the wet cock in his mouth. I started whipping Scott's biceps and his eyes closed while he gurgled and moaned. The cock ring would keep him from coming. It was pure, delicious torture. The beating was invigorating, and both men were scorching.

So why the hell was not I getting aroused?

"Help me lean the chair back," I commanded and Mark stood up, tilting the chair back with Scott aboard. Handing him the cane, I pulled up my skirt, straddling Mark's face with my back to Scott. I knew how good he was at pussy licking and I bore down on his mouth, crushing his tongue into me, rocking back and forth.

"Whip his inner thighs, make him bleed," I said through gnashed teeth, listening to the whistle of the cane as it sliced through the air again and again, slapping hard against Mark's inner thighs.

With my eyes squeezed shut, I saw my couple, fantasizing that I was with them. It was Tiyah's face that I was straddling and it was Elijah that beat her into submission. That got my juices flowing as I ground back and forth against his mouth. Ouch. Razor burn pulled me out of my fantasy and I shot upward so fast that I almost fell forward.

The whipping stopped. "Are you okay?" asked Mark. "What happened?"

"Nothing, I'm fine." I whipped around, catching two spectators standing right inside the doorway. Elijah had leaned up against the wall next to the doorjamb with Tiyah positioned in front of him, facing me. One of his hands was squeezing her breast and the other was buried between her legs. Both sets of eyes were on me. Fuck.

"Excuse me," I said to the two men and approached the couple. Elijah froze, stopping his ministrations, waiting.

"I can't do this," I whispered to them.

"Why not?" Tiyah whined. "We want you."

"Yeah? Well I don't want you." I stormed out of the room, leaving all four people behind.

Chapter Twenty-One

Sunlight burst through my windows, burning holes in my retina at the ungodly hour of ten a.m. Figuratively. Dammit. I'd gotten home so late I'd forgotten to draw my blackout curtains. The sun was harsh and biting, like tiny sand crabs snapping at my bare ankles.

I shifted in bed, restless with unspent energy from the night before, and pressed my hands between my legs, hard against my mound. I had run home last night and gone to sleep without touching myself. My banked fire was burning a hole in my psyche.

Channel your sexual energy into a laser focus. There will be plenty of time to play with yourself later. Or better yet, get someone else to satiate your needs. The problem with that line of thinking was that it led to thoughts of jumping on Tiyah and Elijah. But how could I? I would not be their home-wrecker. How would I be any different from Margery if I destroyed the beautiful relationship they had? My hand flew to my chest. Heartburn? The ache there was new.

The couple wanted me for now, but more likely they were just enamored with the idea of it. The fantasy of a threesome. Of love 'em and leave 'em. Shit, hadn't I perpetuated that exact stereotype for my entire life?

Thumping out to the kitchen in my purple velvet robe and slippers, I found a fresh pot of coffee and a note from Jared. He and Chrys were at their respective schools while the boys had taken Rex out for a walk. I poured myself a cup and sat down at the table, looking at my phone, frowning. Zero messages. Nothing from the couple which, again, was what I wanted, but . . . why hadn't my father called? If I could meet Dad alone and speak to him I was sure we could work things out. He was a lot of things, but racist was not one of them. Dialing his number, I didn't realize I was holding my breath until he answered.

"Maria, hello." His tone was clipped and cold.

"Papa. What are your plans for this morning?"

"Nada. Que?"

"Can you meet me at the cafe on the pier?"

"For breakfast?"

"No, well yeah, I love their pancakes, but mostly

I'd just like to sit somewhere and talk for a bit, if that's okay with you."

"You don't look like you should be eating pancakes, Maria." His chuckle stung. "But I'll meet you. In an hour?"

"That would be great. And, Dad?"

"Yes?"

"Can you come alone, please? I'd like to have a private father-daughter chat."

"Of course." He hung up.

I texted him the name and address before I showered, changed and headed out to the living room. Rex was back with the boys, tail thumping wildly upon seeing me.

"Hey, boy." I ruffled his fur. "Wanna go on another walk?"

He barked up at me.

"Where ya goin'?" Carter asked from the couch, where he sat with Alec, both of them reading on their Kindles.

"To meet my dad at the cafe. I'd ask you two to come along but I need to see him alone."

"Sure, sure." Carter waved a hand at me. "We just got back from there anyway."

"Have fun," called Alec as I let myself and Rex out.

Chapter Twenty-Two

The walk was crisp, the autumn air cool on my face and slightly damp hair. Although it was warm enough out, I found myself shivering in the breeze, wrapping an arm around my body to steady myself. Walking along our ocean bay to the pier steadied my nerves. Surely I could work everything out with my dad, now that he had agreed to come alone. Daddy and his little girl, nothing could come between our relationship. I calmed, focusing on the seagulls calling from the water as they dove and circled. Rex momentarily strained at his leash before falling back in line. He wasn't the only one on a tether.

When I arrived at the Harbor House Cafe, I checked my phone. I was a few minutes early, and I didn't see my father so I chose an outdoor table.

Rex immediately reclined at my feet. I was studying the menu when the sound of a metal chair scraping the wooden planks across from me caused me to look up. Expecting to see my father, I let out a small gurgle when I met Margery's darkening eyes. He was pulling the chair out for her and avoiding my eyes.

"Burgundy." Margery was the only person I'd ever met who could say my name and make it sound ugly. "It was so nice of you to ask us to breakfast."

"Actually, Margery, I needed to discuss some private matters with him."

She waved her hand in front of her face. "Your father and I have no secrets. He wants me here, don't you, dear?"

"She has a good head on her shoulders, this one." He jutted a thumb in her direction and then sat down next to her.

Shit. "Dad, I was hoping to talk to you about the sensitive matter discussed at the Council meeting yesterday, the matter that no one else is supposed to know about."

"Your father has already told me about the were-wolves wanting sanctuary here." She shook out the white cloth napkin but didn't place it on her lap. "Disgusting matter, don't you think?"

"I think it's disgusting that they wouldn't be allowed to take refuge here," I snapped. What the hell? He'd told her about the Council meeting? I hadn't told anyone, not even my two closest friends.

She put her hand up, palm out. "I need some food before we get into this."

Really?

"Waiter." She snapped her fingers at a bus boy who was scurrying by.

He looked over. *"Un minute, senora."*

"Why should I wait? I'm the customer. Bring me some coffee right now."

He hurried off without arguing.

"He's not a waiter."

"I don't care what he is, he can bring me some coffee. He's getting paid to work, isn't he?"

My father sat still without saying a word, and a moment later the bus boy returned with three cups and a coffeepot. He placed one in front of each of us, then poured.

Margery held up her white linen napkin. "Get me a black one, boy."

Heaven forbid she get white lint on her black silk slacks. The busboy took the napkin from her and looked at me, his eyebrows raised. I shrugged and mouthed, "Sorry." Swiftly nodding, he scurried away again, returning quickly with a black linen napkin.

"Cream," Margery snapped.

He ran back with a small silver container and placed it in front of her.

"Sugar," she barked.

The poor kid rolled his eyes.

"Don't you dare roll your eyes at me." Rex stood up and stared at her. "I want to speak to the manager. We are the customers. It's your job to wait on us. You only have one job to do. Is it that difficult?"

"Margery," I kept my voice low and smooth, "this is not his job. His job is to clean the tables."

"Whatever." She waved a hand at him. "Bring me some sugar now."

The boy scurried off again, returning with packets of sugar, which he placed in front of her.

"I'll have the French toast, bacon and a bowl of fruit," she said without looking at him.

He gave me a panicked look and I gave him a tiny nod.

"Dad? Do you want anything?" I asked my father.

"Coffee is fine," he responded.

"I'll be right back." I got up and followed the busboy inside, where I apologized profusely and gave our orders to an actual waiter. Returning to the table, I said, "The food has been ordered."

"Good," said Margery, shaking out the black napkin and placing it on her lap.

I sucked in a breath, trying not to look like a guppy gulping for air. This woman tried my every nerve but what I couldn't figure out yet was if she was doing it on purpose or not. If she was trying to bait me, I would not bite. "So, Dad, I need to talk to you about your role here and the vote."

"What about it?" he asked.

"Well, you were asked to join the Council because you're a Signum-rights lawyer."

"And werewolves are *not* Signum," said Margery hotly.

"Well they're not humans, so actually that does make them Signum. They're supernatural like the rest of us."

"They're uncontrollable creatures," she snapped. "Nothing like us."

"Have you met a werewolf? Talked to any?"

"Of course not." She shook her head. "Why would I do that? They're savages."

"Need I remind you that humans called us savages and worse before we came out?"

"Maria." My father was using his diplomatic tone on me. The same one I used when the discussion was over and I couldn't be swayed. Is this where I'd learned it? Why had I never seen how manipulative it was? I crossed my arms tightly, covering my chest.

"Margery is simply concerned for the safety of all," he said, "humans and Signum alike. It would be irresponsible of us to let a new race into the Edge without knowing if they're volatile or not."

"You don't think they can control themselves? Is

that what this is about?" I asked as the waiter appeared with our food, placing it down before us.

"Thank you," I said, making eye contact with her and smiling.

Margery and my father ignored her completely, but as soon as she walked away, Margery snapped her fingers in the air, pointed to her plate and called out, "This bacon is not cooked to my satisfaction. Bring me another serving that is fully cooked."

My father didn't even seem to notice how rude she was being. Or maybe he didn't care. Was that a proud smile he wore?

"Yes, ma'am, I'm sorry, ma'am," the waiter responded, lifting up the plate.

"Don't be sorry, girl, do your job."

I had to sit on my hands to keep from punching her, reminding myself that my dad found redeeming qualities in her that I had yet to uncover. I cleared my throat and turned toward Dad. "So what you're saying is that you have no idea if werewolves are dangerous or not. You know nothing about them. You've never met one, but you've decided they shouldn't be given a chance?"

"Correct," Margery answered.

"Excuse me but I'm speaking to my father."

He sighed deeply as the woman returned, placed a plate with four strips of well-done bacon next to Margery and hurried away.

Margery pushed the plate aside. "This is worse, it's burnt. No wonder she's only a waitress."

"Darling," he put his hand on her arm, "let it go."

"I'll do no such thing. You know how I feel about letting people get away with things. How will they ever learn or improve? By saying nothing, we simply perpetuate bad behavior. I'm doing them a favor."

"Yes, dear, of course you are. You're right."

"Burgundy, sweetheart," she drawled.

"Yes?"

"The real reason I wanted to be here with your father today was so I could talk to you."

"About?"

"Your future, dear." She took a bite of her pancake, not looking up when one of the waiters refilled her coffee.

"What about my future?"

"Well, your father and I have been talking," she looked at my dad and he nodded, "and we think it's time for you to settle down."

"What does that mean?"

"You're not getting any younger. You are a gorgeous girl." She smiled over at my father. "You obviously got Hervé's handsome looks, but . . . those will fade with time."

"So?"

Margery leaned forward. "You may not always be able to use your beauty to make money, dear."

"Again, so?" I looked at my dad but his face was impassive, watching her.

"Do you mind if I ask how much money you make at the club?" Her tone was light as she blinked her clumpy, mascara-clad lashes at me.

"Most nights I bring in about six fifty." I jutted my chin out. I was proud of my dancing and my earnings.

Margery made an ugly noise in the back of her throat reminiscent of a cat choking up a hairball. "I make six hundred and fifty dollars . . . an hour, dear."

"So what? That makes you better than me?"

She clucked. "I'm sorry, I didn't mean to offend you. I brought that up as a reference. I only desire that you be taken care of." He smiled at my father. "You are daddy's little girl, after all."

Ew. "Again, what the—"

"Maria, please, just hear her out. She has a lot of experience in this area."

"It's my specialty." She offered me a catty grin, like she'd just swallowed someone's pet mouse when they'd turned the other way. "I know about relationships, better than anyone. I can look at a couple and tell you not only if they're going to stay married or get divorced, but also the number of years it'll take." She winked at my father. "That's when I pass out my business cards to the bride or groom at their wedding."

He grinned back at her, his gray eyes sparkling.

Surely she was joking. If she was, it was funny in a very twisted way.

"Women come to me for advice about men on a regular basis, and I'm always right."

My father beamed. "Margery gives her time for free, to help them."

I just bet she does.

"Your father is worried about you." She gazed at him, and he nodded, eyes wide.

"Is this true?" I asked.

"Yes, of course," he said.

"We've discussed it and for your own benefit, we both think that it's time for you to find a man."

"What? A man? What kind of man?" That was nutters.

"A rich, fat, balding, older man." She blinked at me. "You find one of those and you'll be set for life."

I laughed, sure she was joking. "Money can't buy you love."

She and Dad exchanged looks and responded in unison, "Oh yes it can."

No way. They were playing with me, had to be. In a matter of seconds, they'd both jump up and say, "Gotcha!" I leaned back in my chair, determined to let them play it out and have their fun. I'd act surprised when they admitted the gag.

Margery continued, "I'm sure you have your pick

of rich, older men at the strip club. They're probably falling all over you."

Dad nodded on cue. "She's got a point, kiddo. If you marry a rich man, you won't have to strip anymore."

"I love stripping," I bit out before I could curb my tongue. How far were they planning on taking this?

Margery tsked. "What you are doing affects your father's business. I thought you cared more about him." She leaned back. "And, I really hate to play this card but," she sighed deeply, "if you are to be a part of this family, you must properly represent it."

What? She was serious? "Okay, you two, you got me. I'm sorry but I can't play along with this shtick."

"Shtick?" My dad's eyes flashed. He leaned forward, baring his fangs. "This is no joke, Maria. This is your life we are talking about. You're breaking my heart right now!"

"*I'm* breaking *your* heart?" I pushed my chair back. "What's really going on here?" Did this woman have that much power over my father? And the power to cut me out of my own family? Power over his heart *and* his money? If so, I'd gravely underestimated her.

"Whatever do you mean?" She put her hand to her chest, blinking those big, ugly lashes at me again.

"Maria." My father put his hand on my arm, using his vampire strength to pull both me and my chair back toward the table. Pain seared up my arm and I bit down on the inside of my cheek to keep from crying out. The liquid warmth of my own blood seeped down my throat. He'd always been gruff, not realizing his own strength, and as a child I'd had the bruises to prove it. But anytime I'd complained, he'd been surprised, then told me I was too soft and needed to suck it up.

He removed his hand, the outline of his fingers pulsing crimson against my skin. "Please don't be so difficult. Margery is the most caring woman I know. She wants to make all of our lives better."

Bullshit. The stench of this woman's manipulation overpowered me, my knuckles whitening as I gripped the sides of my chair.

"Burgundy, darling," she drawled, "please think about all of this. We're not asking you to make a decision right away."

"A decision? About what?" My nostrils flared, eyes narrowing. Looking at her without flipping the table was becoming a challenge.

"Whether you want to remain in your father's life or not."

I turned to my father, but he said nothing, running his hand over his face.

"I don't understand what's going on here. So

you're saying if I don't marry a rich man, you won't love me anymore?"

He rolled his eyes. "Always so dramatic."

Margery drummed her perfectly manicured fingers on the table. "Two things, dear. I'll spell them out for you. First of all, we want you to explain to your boss how bad it would be for the citizens of the Edge if he were to allow werewolves in, and secondly . . ." She picked up her water and took a long swallow. "We'd like you to stop stripping and settle down. I suggested a rich man because, let's be realistic here, your dad can't keep supporting you forever."

I shook my head to clear it. Did this woman have something on my dad? Or over him? The man was no pushover. Why would he let her dictate what he did with his money? It was *his* to do with as he pleased. And why would he care that I was a stripper? Didn't he used to visit strippers himself? Back in Nicaragua? Obviously he cared more about what this woman thought than his own daughter. Well, fuck them. I didn't need his money, and if his love had suddenly become conditional, I could live without that as well.

Margery cleared her throat. "Think about it, dear, that's all I'm saying. With your father on the Council and working here as a prominent lawyer, it looks bad to have a daughter slumming it."

"Not as bad as it looks to have a cunt for a wife."

Chapter Twenty-Three

Walking down to the end of the boardwalk afterward, I wanted to vomit. What an awful woman. My father had tried to make me apologize but I'd refused and Margery had claimed she respected a woman who wasn't afraid to speak her mind.

Then she'd become even more belligerent to the waitstaff, demanding that the cost of her entire breakfast be removed from the bill because the food was "tasteless." I'd been eating at the Harbor for years and their food was delicious. They had hundreds of four- and five-star Yelp reviews and had been voted the best breakfast spot in the Edge five years in a row. I had the feeling this woman would even complain about a three-star Michelin restaurant.

What the hell was going on with my father? How could I fix this? Suddenly he was a racist. Or was he just acting that way to placate *her*?

Stopping to let Rex do his business, I pulled out my phone and called Benedict.

"Burgundy." His sharp British accent flooded the line. "What can I do for you?"

"It doesn't look like my father is going to help with werewolf rights. Is it too late to replace him on the Council?"

"He was voted in," Benedict said. "And no one can be replaced until either their term is up or they quit on their own."

"What happens now?"

"We meet next week, and each member will present their arguments, and then we'll vote again."

"And if it's still a tie?"

"We'll have to bring in all past members of the council that still live in the Edge, and they will be the deciding factor."

"Is there any way that could end up in a tie?"

"I've looked through the list and no, it's an uneven number but . . ."

"What?" I continued walking with Rex, not even able to enjoy the glittering ocean waves.

"Nothing like that has ever happened before. We'd be in new territory."

"Great."

"I wish I could predict the outcome, or that I had more leverage over everyone, but the Council was created to debate and decide contentious issues just like these."

"Yeah."

My one-word responses gave me away.

He chuckled. "Hey, cheer up, I've got a good feeling about this."

"I hope so." I hung up. His optimism surprised me. If that stately curmudgeon could look on the bright side, why couldn't I? Probably because my father was on the Council, voting it down. But was it really my dad talking or was it that woman's voice coming out of his mouth?

"Burgundy?" A familiar voice rang out and I looked up to see Elijah walking out of a shop.

Tension hung thick in the air like a dense fog blanketing the bay. I was torn between sprinting the other way without responding or throwing my arms around him to cry and bury my face in his chest. What's behind door number three? Deal with this situation like the responsible grown-up I was.

"Elijah . . ." My heart rate increased and I flushed, my hands moistening. When was I ever at a loss for words, let alone besieged by nerves? "About the other night."

He waited, head cocked.

"I apologize." I held his gaze. "I was undeniably rude to the both of you."

He dipped his chin. "Apology accepted, thank you. We were all at fault, really. Emotions were high. We should have asked for your permission, respected your wishes and not thrown ourselves on you. But can you blame us?" He offered me a lopsided grin. "So is that why you came here? To apologize?"

"I wish I could say yes, but no. I had a difficult," I looked back down the pier, squinting, "brunch. I was walking to clear my head. I didn't know you worked" —I looked at the sign above the door—"at the Barnacle."

He visibly softened, the tension easing out of his body. "Ah, so then you didn't come to take me up on the dive lessons either?"

"Dive lessons?"

He pointed. Stenciled on the window was *Diving Lessons, Rentals, Snorkeling.*

"I've never even stepped inside this place."

He shrugged. "Want a tour?"

"Sure. Can I bring Rex inside?"

"All are welcome." He pointed to a dog's water bowl outside the shop.

"Won't I get you in trouble with your boss?"

A grin stretched across his face, lighting up those pale-blue eyes. "Probably not."

Relief washed over me in a wave. After the abysmal conversation with my dad and Margery, Elijah's grudgeless open heart was a beacon on a moonless night.

The shop was immaculate, which surprised me since I had assumed that Elijah and Tiyah had never invited me over to their boat because it was cramped and dirty. Maybe another employee cleaned the shop or the boss was a stickler.

Looking around, I ran my fingers over some of the snorkeling equipment without paying attention and ran full force into a very solid chest.

"Well, hello there," came a deep voice.

Elijah was next to me in a flash. "Jonas, this is my friend Burgundy. Burg, my brother, Jonas."

I backed away to extend my hand. He brought it up to his mouth for a kiss. These Aaron brothers were slick.

"I didn't know you had a brother."

Elijah grinned. "You and I don't do much talking."

Jonas dropped my hand, clearing his throat and looking between us. "So has your friend met your wife yet?"

He was protective of Tiyah. I liked that. "I know her well. Better than I know your brother."

Jonas nodded, apparently satisfied with my response.

"You," I tapped his rock-hard chest, "look familiar."

Elijah snorted. "Not a very original line, Burg."

I rolled my eyes at him, then went back to staring at Jonas. I'd seen him recently. But where? At the V?

"So tell me," I leaned against the shelves, "how do brothers end up working together at the same dive shop? Do you know the owner?"

Jonas made eye contact with Elijah again, who merely shrugged and said, "You could say that."

"She doesn't know?" asked Jonas.

"Know what?"

"Elijah and I *are* the owners."

I almost knocked over the shelves in my surprise. "What? You never told me that."

"Again . . . not a lot of talking." He winked at me.

"Okay, what the hell is going on here?" Jonas asked. "I feel like I should call Tiyah and tell her."

"Please do," said Elijah and handed his phone to his brother.

I looked at him questioningly. "Can we speak, in private?"

"Sure, follow me to the office." Elijah walked to the back of the store. I followed with Rex after offering Jonas a wan smile. His jaw was working as he glared at us with eyes a shade darker than his brother's.

Once in the office I shut the door. "What the

hell? Do you want your brother to find out? Are you completely uninterested in discretion?"

He shrugged and sat down in a chair. "My brother's cool but it'd be best if he heard it from Tiyah and not from me."

"Heard what?"

"About our arrangement."

"We don't have an arrangement, Elijah. We've had some fun together." A lot of fun. "But that's all. Sex is meaningless."

"Can you look me in the eyes and tell me you don't have feelings for us?"

"Feelings? I have sexual stirrings for both of you. I like you a lot as people. Friends. Friends I fuck even. I'm not sure what you're asking."

"You don't feel anything more for us?"

Fuck. I shook my head. "If you want to have a conversation like this, Tiyah needs to be here too."

"I'll call her."

"And we probably shouldn't do it while you're at work."

"We'll come over later."

"Elijah . . ."

He looked so vulnerable, those blue eyes searching mine. Something welled up in my chest, something a lot like when Sadie or Jared was hurting or sad. Well, that was unexpected. I wanted to hold him and kiss him, but I couldn't. Not without Tiyah, not without an understanding. And damn me if I didn't want it.

"Yes," I finally said. "Let's all talk later."

He nodded those lovely flaxen curls. "She wants there to be an us."

"An us?"

"Yes."

"You mean all three of us?"

"Yes."

"Are you proposing a triad?" Fantasy is always better than reality.

He shrugged. "Is that what it's called? I just know that we're both completely smitten with you and we can't imagine our relationship continuing without you in it."

"Whoa." I held my hand up. "This is too much for me to process right now." I pushed the jolt of loneliness, the allure of belonging to someone, away. I had to. What he offered could never work.

"Okay, take whatever time you need. If you want to wait a few days to talk, we'll wait."

"Rex, come." I opened the office door and the dog followed me out. Jonas was on the phone.

"Okay, I just wanted to make sure everything was copacetic."

I rounded the corner and watched him. He stood tall with a wide stance, head held high. Protective?

"You're my sister too, Tiyah, and as pack leader, I have to watch out for everyone."

Pack leader? That's where I'd seen him before. He was the new shifter on the Council. He looked very different here, wearing shorts and a tank with wisps of wild curls. Untamed. Without the suit he also looked much younger. But this was the same man. I rushed back to the office just as Elijah was coming out.

"I thought you said you weren't Signum?" I threw at him.

"Huh?"

"Your brother was at the Council meeting the other day. Benedict told me he's the new shifter that replaced someone who moved away. I'd ask if you were adopted, but the similarity between you two is uncanny. Care to explain?"

He looked down but not before fear flashed in his eyes. "I can't." He reached for my hand, then clutched it to his heart when I didn't pull away. "Do you trust me?"

"Trust is earned."

"Please, Burgundy."

"Please what?"

"Don't say anything to Benedict yet. Give us a little more time. We'll explain when we can. I promise."

"And the *we* that you're referring to?"

"Tiyah. Me. Jonas."

"You have a week."

He let out a long breath. "I understand. Can we still see you tonight? To talk about us?"

"How can there be an us when you're obviously hiding something major from me?"

Chapter Twenty-Four

I was getting ready for work when the doorbell rang. Rex started to bark.

"I'll get it," Chrys called. A few minutes later there was a knock on my bedroom door.

I opened it to Chrys standing in the hallway, looking a little confused. "Your dad's here. He asked me to get you."

"Okay. Tell him I'll be right out." That was strange. Was he going to tell me off?"

I threw on the rest of my outfit and marched out to the living room, where he sat on one of the wing-back chairs.

Rising, he took my hand in his and kissed each cheek. "It's important to me that you get along with my wife."

I sat across from him, narrowing my eyes, keeping my mouth clamped shut.

"The thing you have to understand about Margery is that she is the most amazing person I've ever known . . . in every way."

This threw me off but I was willing to try, for him. "How so?" I leaned forward.

"She is kind, thoughtful, intelligent, and she continually challenges me."

"Kind? I don't understand. From what I've seen she's judgmental and rude."

"It's her armor. An act. She has a difficult time shedding her lawyerly persona but she lets her guard down with me. I see her for who she truly is, the kindest and most caring person I know."

Ouch and bafflement. Was he deluded or did he really believe that? Or did he *have* to believe it? I knew over a dozen people who were nicer than Margery—my mother and I for two. Being mean for self-protection or for any reason at all still counts as being mean. "So how does she challenge you?" Maybe that was the key to this puzzle.

He laughed. "She will argue about anything and everything. I love that. And there's no way you can win, even if you're right and she's wrong. Because if she senses she's losing, she'll make things up to win the argument. Fake facts. And the funniest part is you don't know if what she's saying is true or false."

His laughter was deep and rumbling. Utterly disturbing. I shivered.

"So she'll flat out lie to win an argument, even if she's wrong?"

"I love that about her." His lips slid up, the smile stretching across his handsome face. "Keeps me on my toes."

"But . . ."

He got up and rearranged himself next to me on the couch, reaching out to pat me on the back. "I don't expect you to understand, Maria. You've never been in love."

Ouch. And untrue. But how would he know? He never wanted to. Did he prefer to see me as an extension of himself? Someone he could control?

"Dad, I really don't get this. You're telling me that you're blinded by a woman who has no integrity?"

"Why would you think she has no integrity? Haven't you been listening? I told you, she is the kindest, most amazing woman I've ever known."

Why did that feel like a stake to the heart? I let out a breath of air I hadn't realized I'd been holding, and he held up a hand.

"If you can't be happy for me . . ." He shook his head, wearing a hurt look. Manipulation.

"I'm happy that you're happy." It was all I could manage.

"Now we just need to find you an honest career

and a rich husband. After all, you're almost fifty. It's time for you to get your life together."

The hell? I was still in my early forties and what did my age have to do with anything? I'd had my life together at eighteen, my first job at fourteen. "Is that you or Margery talking?"

"She only wants what's best for you and for me."

"What does she have on you, Dad?"

He leaned back, folding his arms across his broad chest. "I'm in love with this woman, Maria. A deep love I never knew was even possible. I believe that she has your best interests at heart, she just has a different way of communicating that. Can you trust me on this?"

No. But for my house and everyone who counted on me, I held my tongue. I may have acted like a big, bad wolf earlier when I told my father that I didn't need his money, but the reality of it actually disappearing caused my palms to sweat. Not for myself, I could live in a van if need be, but for my friends. I was the den mother. I couldn't forsake them. *My* pack.

Chapter Twenty-Five

The thumping music that night at the V was already giving me a headache. The dim lights seemed so bright I shielded my eyes, not able to focus on anything above the din of talking, clinking glasses and that music. Maybe I could slip out and just go home.

"Burgundy?" Jared was standing in front of me, wearing a concerned expression.

"*Sí*," I answered without thinking.

"What's wrong?" He touched my shoulder.

"Is it that obvious?"

"Yeah," he chuckled, "I know you better than anyone, remember?"

"I wouldn't want to forget. Hug?"

"Wow, this is serious." He pulled me in, weaving those strong arms around my back, and I leaned into his chest. Wrapped up in his warm scent of Paco Rabanne cologne, I let the familiar notes of grapefruit, leather and mint calm me.

"Do you want to talk about it?"

I shook my head against him. "I do have a question though."

"Shoot."

"Do shifters form packs?"

He pushed me out to arm's length. "Sometimes. Why?"

"Just something I heard the other day. Why aren't you in one?"

His amber eyes flickered. "I guess you could say that Alec and I are in one. Shifters often refer to their family members as their pack. When I was growing up, my parents used the term for me and Sam."

"Doesn't it originally come from werewolves?"

Jared bit back a laugh. "Werewolves? Where did that come from? Sure, in fiction—books and movies —but in reality? You know there's no such thing."

"Yeah." I reached up and kissed his cheek. "One more thing. Would you ever call someone in your family the pack leader?"

"We didn't, but I guess maybe my dad could have held that role." He couldn't hide the pain in his eyes.

I had to stop talking about this with him. When he was eighteen, his parents had been brutally murdered by Trackers, a fanatical religious group bent on wiping out Signum.

"So are you here for Alec tonight?"

He nodded, biting his lip.

"I bet he wishes the circus was open all year round so he could perform there instead."

Jared's face brightened. "Totally. He much prefers working there."

"The atmosphere is very different." I barked out a laugh. If there were another place I could dance half naked, reveling in my sexual power, I'd do it too. But circuses and strippers didn't really mix. The kiddies and all.

"Want to get a drink? I have a while before Alec goes on."

"Sure."

"The usual?" Carter asked us and we sat down at the bar together. We nodded, then turned to watch a lively girl bounce around on stage.

"Jared? One last question."

"Yeah?"

"Can shifters bond to more than person?"

He shook his head. "Not that I know of. Why so many shifter questions, Burgundy?"

"Just curious."

"I know you way better than that but I'll let it go . . . for now. So, you still doing doubles dancing with Tiyah?"

"We are. The crowd seems to love it."

He laughed. "What's not to love."

Carter returned with our drinks and slid them over to us. "Hey, Burg?"

"Yeah?" I turned around.

"Isn't that your dad?" He pointed toward the front door.

My father stood just inside the entrance, blinking at the stage, a sly grin on his face. Ew. "Be right back, guys." I slid off my barstool and approached my father. "Hey, Dad."

He spun toward me, wearing a look of complete surprise. Weird. "Maria, I didn't expect to see you here."

"This is where I work."

"Yes. Yes of course."

"So, where's your *lovely* wife?" My voice oozed sarcasm.

"Margery and Deenie are home tonight, playing mah-jongg." He shrugged. "It's Margery's favorite game."

Of course it was. "And you're here because . . . ?"

"Oh, right." He straightened his tie. "I'm meeting Amber for," he looked around, "a drink."

"A drink at the bar or a drink from her?"

He grinned at me. "A drink from her."

I rustled up a thin-lipped smiled. "I don't know how you do things back in Nicaragua, but I have four donors so that no one needs a blood transfusion."

"Well I'm new here and I haven't gone shopping yet."

"You can always go to a vectum."

He laughed. "Me? A vectum? You never know what you're getting there. Besides, I prefer to have a . . . connection with my donors."

My father and I hadn't ever talked about this. I'd left home when I was eighteen, and as a minor, my dad had procured my donors for me. "Me too. You could always take out an ad and interview for more."

"I'll consider it." He was looking around, presumably for Amber.

"Where are you two meeting?"

"She said to come to a back room, that we'd have more privacy there."

"Right. Follow me." I led my dad to the sex rooms, which was weird, but vampires often used them for drinking too. The "V" stood for vampire, after all. Sure enough, Amber was waiting for him in one of the rooms I peeked into. "Hey, Amber."

"Hey, Burgundy." She offered me a huge smile.

"I brought my dad. He said he was meeting you here?"

"Yep, thanks," she called out, waving at him. "Hi, Hervé, nice to see you."

Dad entered, looking around. "What kind of

room is this?" He was eyeing the bed with raised brows.

"They're . . . intimacy rooms, but we can use them for drinking too," I replied.

"I see. Okay then. Thank you, Maria." He waved me away.

"Great. Welcome. Enjoy." I left them. On my way back to the bar, I saw Benedict.

"Hi, Burgundy. Enjoying your night?"

"Not yet." I winked at him and he laughed.

"Soon enough, I hope."

I waggled my eyebrows at him. "Hey, can we talk for a minute?"

"Sure. Here or in my office?"

"Your office. Please."

I followed him up the stairs near the front door of the club and into his spacious office. He motioned for me to sit in the chair facing away from the monitors, then sat down opposite and tilted his head at me.

"How well do you know the new shifter on the Council?"

"Jonas?"

I nodded.

"Not well. He moved here recently, why?"

"Did he get a blood test?"

"A Signum blood test?"

"Yeah."

"Of course. We wouldn't allow a Signum on the Council without testing them first."

"And he passed as a shifter?"

"Yes." He cocked his head again. "Why?"

"There was nothing out of the ordinary with his test?"

Benedict took in a deep breath and held it, his brows pulling tight. "There was an anomaly. Our Signum doctor said it's a mutation that shows up sometimes. He's seen it before and assured me it was nothing to be concerned about. But now that you're asking, I'm getting concerned."

I waved my hand about. "I'm sure it's nothing. I'm not a geneticist, after all." I laughed. "Did you know that Elijah is his brother?"

"I did, yes. Why?"

"Just wondering." I flashed him a placating smile, one that didn't reach my eyes, and stood up. "Thanks for the chat."

"That's it?"

"That's it." I made my way back to the bar where Jared was saving my seat.

"Perfect timing," he said loudly, the music drowning out his voice. He pointed to the stage where Alec was entering.

A few minutes later, we were so engrossed in Alec's set that I barely registered Amber running out from the back and zooming out the front door. I found it strange that she didn't stop to say goodbye, but she must have been in a hurry to get somewhere. Then my father emerged from the back as well, a strange look on his face. Anger? He approached me and grabbed my arm, hard.

"What's going on?" I said crossly.

"You tell me," he growled.

"Excuse me?" I tried to pull my arm away but he held onto it tightly, leaning into my ear.

"What the fuck is that?"

"What the fuck is what?"

"That thing you had me drink from?"

"Amber?"

"Obviously, Maria. What the fuck is it?"

"I'm not following, Dad."

"That's no woman."

Whoa. "What?"

"That thing is a man."

I wrenched my arm free. "First of all, she's not a thing. She's a person, and second of all, she's all woman."

"Not with a dick she's not."

"And how would you know she has a dick?"

"You disgust me. You know that? I did not raise you to be a stripper. I did not raise you to talk back to me. I did not raise you to be friends with *she-males*," he spat. "Margery was right about you after all."

Chapter Twenty-Six

After my father stormed out, I sat on the barstool in shock. Jared turned to me after Alec left the stage.

"Burgundy, what's wrong? You're white as bone."

"I . . . I'll be right back." I slid off the stool and went to the room my dad and Amber had been in. Sitting down on the bed, I called her. She didn't answer. I texted. *What happened with my dad? You ok?*

No response. Shit. What the hell had happened? I looked around the room and then got up and looked in the trashcan. Discarded used condoms and wrappers. Could be from anyone. Setting my jaw, I made my way back to Benedict's office and knocked lightly on the door.

"Who is it?"

"Me, Burgundy."

"Come in."

I entered to see a folder spread open on his desk. He looked up, closing it. "Is everything all right?"

"Can you do me a favor?"

"Depends on what it is."

"I know you run video in the sex rooms. I need to look at one."

"That's overstepping policy. Those tapes are kept for the police, only to be viewed by law enforcement in cases of an alleged forced encounter or drug use." He sounded like he was reciting from a manual.

"I know, Ben. But I need this. There may have been a forced encounter that someone isn't going to report."

"Who?"

I took a very deep, long breath. "My father."

He shook his head quickly. "What?"

"My father and Amber, in the blue room. Twenty minutes ago. Please."

Benedict rolled to his monitors and punched in several codes on a keypad. A minute later, a black and white video popped up and there they were, talking. It looked like right after I had left. Amber was still seated in the chair and Dad was standing. "Do you need the sound?"

"Please."

He turned a knob and brought it up.

"I didn't think you'd be calling me again so soon, Mr. Rosales."

"Well, I liked what I drank and I want another taste. Can you blame me?"

She laughed nervously. *"And you're fine with paying the same amount?"*

"Five hundred, correct?"

"Yes, sir. Thank you." She held out her hand and my father counted out five one hundred-dollar bills.

It was a standard rate for multiple drinks within a month from a high-quality donor. And I knew Amber needed the money for her surgery.

"Were would you like me?"

My father looked around the room. *"Would you be comfortable on the bed?"*

Amber looked anything but. *"Of course."* Her voice was higher pitched than usual. She crossed over and sat down on the edge.

My father sat next to her and gently moved her hair back from her neck, then moved forward to bite her. When his fangs sank into her throat, she gasped and threw her head back. He wrapped his hands around her shoulders and held her there, drinking. The whites of her eyes showed and she let out a moan. Immediately one of his hands moved down to her breast. Not cool at all. She didn't move and I watched as my own father groped my friend and lover. I wanted to look away but I couldn't.

"She can report that," Benedict bit out. "If she didn't want him to do that, he can be prosecuted."

I didn't respond and we kept watching as my father's hands moved over her body, grabbing her other breast, and then down to her waist and back up again. Finally he cradled the side of her face and detached, licking his lips.

"You are delicious." He smiled at her.

"Thank you." She reddened and stood up.

"Wait. Please." He pulled on her arm and she sat down again, looking over at him.

"Yes? Is there something else?"

My father removed his wallet and pulled out several more hundreds. *"I was wondering if you'd be interested in making some more money?"*

She eyed the wad. *"What do I have to do for it?"*

His eyes moved to her mouth and he pointed at his crotch. Eww. No fucking way. I mean, I knew my dad was a pervert, but . . .

"I can't watch this."

"Turn around, I'll watch."

"Is your wife okay with this?" Amber asked.

"What she doesn't know won't hurt her. Besides," his voice was soft, cajoling, *"oral sex isn't cheating."*

Really? I gagged at the sounds that soon followed. "Turn it down or off, please. Or fast-forward. Or something," I begged.

"Sorry, sorry." Benedict turned off the volume as I grabbed a nearby trashcan and vomited into it.

"Shit," he said a few minutes later.

"What?"

"I have to rewind and turn up the volume. Do you want to leave?"

"Is his dick back in his pants?"

"Yeah."

I turned around as Benedict rewound several frames and played the tape. He was zipping up and they both stood, my father's gaze moving down to Amber's crotch. *"I bet that got you all wet."*

She didn't meet his eye. *"It was hot, sir, yes."* Her cheeks reddened and my father pulled out his wallet and took out several more bills.

"I want to touch your pussy." He handed her the money but she didn't take it.

"No, sir, thank you. I'd rather not."

With lightning vampire speed, my father had her on her back on the bed, his palm over her crotch, pushing. *"What's this?"*

"Get off me!" She twisted and screamed but he was much stronger and had forced her dress up.

"You're shy. How sweet." He pulled at the bindings between her legs, holding her down with his other hand.

"Stop it," she cried as he worked the fabric free.

The look on his face was grotesque as her penis, semi-hard, sprang free.

"What the hell is this?" he yelled. *"What the fuck are you?"*

Amber turned her head away, tears spilling from her eyes.

"You disgust me," he hissed.

I was about to look away and insist that Benedict stop the tape when Amber stood up. She teetered for only a moment. Regaining her balance, she fixed her outfit and stood her ground, jaw set, head held high. Good for her.

"You're the one who's disgusting." The rumble of her voice was low, menacing.

He held his hand out. *"Give me back my money . . . man-whore."*

"I earned this money." She turned toward the door but my father grabbed her arm, and from the shriek she let out, I knew it was as hard as he often grabbed mine. Spinning her back around to face him, his other hand shot out, presumably to take the money from her. But Amber was trained in self-defense. With all the homophobes in the Edge, she'd told me, she had no choice. And in one beautiful, balletic movement, her knee met his crotch.

My father bellowed and doubled over, and Amber ran out the door.

Chapter Twenty-Seven

I sat in my bedroom, crying into Rex's fur. Amber wouldn't answer any of my texts, and why would she? How could he? Was this the kind of man my father had always been and I'd just been too blind to see it? Too blinded with love? *Daddy's girl* rang in my ears. The words that used to make me beam with pride now made me cringe in disgust. What if this had been a one-off? *You're obviously skilled at lying to yourself, Burg, but that's too ridiculous even for you to believe.* And why would that matter anyway? One time was once too many. Fuck. I couldn't even protect my favorite human donor. From my own father.

My phone buzzed with a text and I lunged for it, hoping it was Amber. It was Tiyah.

We need to see you. Please. Elijah told me what happened today. Can we talk? Or just cuddle?

Shit, I could use a cuddle. *Come over, I'm at home.*

I got up, unlocked the front door for them and then forced myself to shower. When I stepped out of the bathroom in a robe, the house smelled like vanilla, and Tiyah was walking out of the kitchen carrying a tray of tea.

"Hi." She grinned. "You look good enough to eat."

I forced a smile in return and her eyes widened.

"What's wrong?"

"Nothing. I'm glad you're here."

"Something's wrong. I can tell but I won't push it. Elijah's waiting in the living room."

"Thank you, and you're right, but I don't want to talk about it yet." She knew me almost as well as my besties, which scared the blood right out of me. I followed her, finding her husband sitting on the couch reading a magazine. A surge of warmth coursed through me. They'd made themselves comfortable here. In my house.

"Burgundy," he said when we entered and rose to kiss my cheek, taking the tray from his lady and putting it down on the coffee table. He motioned for me to sit next to him and she sat on my other side. "What's wrong?" he asked, concerned.

Geez, I obviously could not hide my anguish from these two.

"She doesn't want to talk about it," Tiyah said.

"Is it us?" he asked.

"No. No, it's something else. Look. I'm happy to see you two but I'm not really in a talking place."

"Oh?" said Elijah. "I thought you wanted us to come over. Did we misunderstand?"

"Tiyah offered a cuddle," I said. "And that I could definitely use."

They both broke into smiles and put their arms around me.

"Let's go into the bedroom." I stood, motioning for them to follow me. "And grab the tea."

In my room we disrobed and climbed into my bed to sip our tea without talking. Then, keeping me in the middle they both wrapped their bodies around me like a cocoon. That, I could get used to. I hadn't felt this safe since Sadie and Jared had found their mates.

The next morning burst through my eyelids as bright sunlight glinted through the windows. I'd forgotten to draw my curtains. Again. Tiyah and Elijah still held me wrapped up between them and I studied their faces basked in the light. My breath caught at the way it highlighted Tiyah's lovely dark hair and shimmered off Elijah's stark-white curls. The rays caressed both of my lovers and like magic hour, it made them look as though they were movie stars just stepping onto a set. Their sheer beauty over-whelmed even me. These two had become more than mere lovers, people who occasionally graced my bed. Somehow, without my vigilance, they had found their way into my heart. It was one of the many reasons I rarely slept with anyone more than twice, besides my donors, Sadie or Ryder. Jared and I used to be inti-mate at times, but when he'd bonded to Alec it had stopped and I respected that. Plus he wasn't bisexual and had only done it to please me, which had some-times seemed forced.

But these two. Tiyah, with her full lips and sepia-toned skin, completely unblemished, those long, dark lashes resting on her cheeks. Turning my head the other way, I was met with the contrast of Elijah's ruddy skin and tight, blond curls. I didn't enjoy one more than the other. They were the perfect pair. Yin and yang. But could they be *my* yin and yang? And what did that make me? Ying? Yan? Yiang? Or maybe not defining it was okay too. Elijah's eyes flitted open and he smiled widely, pulling himself toward me and burying his face in my neck. His top arm, which was lying over my chest, reached for Tiyah and he stroked her over me. She stirred and did the same, nuzzling into my neck and petting him over me.

"Why don't I go make us all some coffee," she said, sleep lacing her voice.

"That'd be great, babe," he said.

She got up and leaned down to kiss both of us on the lips, first me and then him, her hand disappearing under the sheets.

He groaned a moment later, closing his eyes, and she leaned back down to kiss me while fisting his cock. Her lips were soft and warm as they parted my mouth.

"You know what I'd like to happen while I'm making coffee?" she whispered, pulling away from my lips.

No one said anything as she hovered above me, her hand still on him.

"I want you two to make love while I'm not here. I want to walk in on you with the coffee already made and either watch you fucking or see you both satiated."

He kept groaning as she played with him. Watching for signs of duress or upset, I asked, "Why?"

"Shhh." She leaned down and kissed me again. "If this is going to work the way I want it to, the way I know Elijah wants it to, we have to have sex with you without one another. I love the idea of it but I need it to happen to be sure. Does that make sense?"

His eyes popped open and he sucked in his bottom lip. "It does to me."

I had to admit that it made sense to me too. In a proper triad it was rarely all three people all the time;

I didn't know anyone who had ever done that. A threesome now and again, yes, but a triad was different. It meant we were all equal lovers, one big "thruple," and for that to happen, every party had to be fine with sex between the others. I nodded at her.

"Good." Her smile warmed me. She kissed each of us, let go of him, grabbed one of my robes and traipsed out of the bedroom, closing the door behind her.

Elijah rolled on his side, facing me. "How does this work? You're a Domme and I'm a Dom."

"I can swing both ways and I know you can too. Would you prefer I take the lead?"

"Whatever makes you—"

I rolled my body on top of his, stopping his words with my mouth, grinding myself into his hardness. His hands wandered over my body, tugging at my breasts, pulling one into his mouth and sucking on my nipple. Biting and teasing it with his teeth and tongue. I thrust against him, then sat up, popping my tit out of us mouth. I swung my leg over the bed, taking his hand and pulling him with me.

"Let's make sure she can see us when she comes back." I moved to the end of the bed, got down on my knees and kneeled over the mattress, ass in the air.

"Yes," he hissed, dropping on all fours behind me

where he buried his face in my ass and pussy, licking and probing me with his tongue.

I rocked back into him as he spread me open, plunging two fingers inside of me and pumping them deep. With his other hand, he pinched and rolled my clit between thumb and forefinger.

"Fuck me, Elijah," I moaned into the comforter. My head turned to the side, my entire body rigid. "Give me that cock."

"In your pussy or in your ass?"

Ohh, *choices* . . .

"Condom," I gurgled and he jumped up to grab one from my dresser drawer, returning with lube and a dildo.

"You took too long to answer so the decision is mine," he said playfully, positioning himself over me and squirting lube onto my ass. He massaged it in and pressed at my gate while alternately fingering me and playing with my clit.

I tried to press my ass back, to force him inside, but he held me still with surprisingly strong hands—one on either side of my ass.

I jolted forward as his cock breached my ring, just the tip of it, but he buried his fingers inside of me, stroking until I relaxed. Then he replaced his fingers with a large dildo that worked my pussy while hitting my clit.

"Oh fuck yes," I groaned and he pressed his cock

in further as I bucked back into him, taking it all. My pleasure grew quickly as his cock pumped inside my ass and the dildo filled my pussy. "Fuck me, Elijah, yes like that," I screamed, more so Tiyah could hear than for him or myself. The thought of her listening outside the door threw me over the edge and my orgasm gushed from deep inside my core, radiating outward in heated convulsions. While I bucked and squirmed like a wild horse, Elijah held his ground, driving into me and screaming out my name as he came inside of me. I thrashed and screamed, garbled words and he did the same, holding onto me, riding me hard until I collapsed forward and he collapsed on top of me, sweaty and panting.

The door opened almost immediately and Tiyah entered, putting the tray of coffee down on my night-stand and then getting onto the bed. We looked up at her. I was worried, and I was sure he was as well. He was still inside of me, for god's sake.

The enormous smile spreading across her face told us all we needed to hear.

Chapter Twenty-Eight

We all stayed in bed until late morning, pleasing one another, drinking coffee and talking. By the time they went back to their boat, I'd convinced myself this relationship could work. And after they left, I immediately wanted them to come back.

Instead, I called Amber again and again. She didn't answer, so I sent her a text, keeping it diplomatic. How would she feel if she knew I'd witnessed the entire scene? Invasion of privacy much?

Hi, I'm worried about you. Please let me know if you're okay, and if not, I'm here for you. I'm loyal to you first.

Then I called Iphigenia and asked her to meet me at the Harbor House Cafe. No doubt I'd have to apologize profusely to the waitstaff there as well.

Geez, my dad and his female prison guard sure were leaving an ugly wake.

After showering and dressing, I made my way down to the boardwalk with Rex.

Iphi was waiting for me outside, pert and pretty at a table for two. She rose to greet me and pet the pooch, kissing his face over and over.

"I ordered you some tea and your favorite breakfast, pancakes and bacon." Those big blue eyes batted. "I'm honestly surprised that you asked to meet me. I don't think we've ever hung out alone, just the two of us."

I licked my lips. "I don't think we have either. But I didn't know who else to talk to."

"About?"

"Some personal issues."

"Why not talk to Sadie or Jared?"

"They're both so full with their own lives and I need an unbiased ear. Someone who doesn't know my family dynamics."

She leaned her elbows on the table, cradling her chin in her hands. "That'd be me, all right." Those big, blue eyes blinked at me under a thick mane of blond, corkscrew curls. "I'm all ears and I'm honored that you chose me. I've always wanted to spend time with you."

"You have?"

"Sure. You're Sadie's best friend and Chrys's

roommate. I'm the only witchy sister that hasn't had any alone time with you."

"Ha. Well, I wish it were under better circumstances."

The waiter brought the food and tea. Iphigenia leaned back in her chair to spread her napkin across her lap and then leaned forward again, focusing completely on me.

"Iphi, I have a few things I need to say. In confidence."

"You can trust me."

"I know I can. You've kept confidences for both your sisters in the past. It's the other reason I came to you."

She nodded, waiting.

I told her about what had happened with my dad and Amber at the club, in detail. I'd never spoken about anything even remotely sexual with Iphi, but she was nineteen, and though she never flaunted her sexuality the way Sadie did, I got the feeling she wasn't anywhere near as innocent as Chrys had been at twenty-five. And the one thing I knew about Iphi for sure was that she wasn't judgmental. I told her about my dad's new squeeze and how condescending and passive-aggressive Margery had been with me. How I suspected her of trying to push me out of my own family.

I gauged her reactions throughout and the only

telltale sign were her eyes. Sometimes they widened and other times her brows drew tight in concern.

When I was finished she reached across the table and took my hand over my plate, fork and all.

"Oh, Burgundy, I'm so sorry."

"Thank you for saying that. I just don't get it. My dad isn't who I thought he was and maybe I always knew he was an ass. I mean . . ."

"You don't have to explain that to me. Look at my mother."

I nodded. Aurelia and my father had a lot in common. "This is difficult to believe, let alone say, but Margery makes Aurelia look like Mary fucking Poppins."

Iphi laughed so hard that the water she had just been drinking squirted out of her nose. She brought her napkin up to her face, still giggling.

"Speaking of, are your mom and Alistair still together?"

"They are. It's so weird. Such an unlikely pair."

"Yeah, who knows anymore what someone else is attracted to."

"Is there something else?"

"Besides my new, evil stepmonster and perverted, rapist, asshole father?"

She nodded solemnly, waiting.

"And you say you don't know me well. Am I that easy to read?"

Her plump, pink lips stretched into a wide grin. "Not at all but you forget, I've lived around you for most of my life. I was fifteen when Sadie met you and moved in with you and Jared. I'm observant.

That I did not doubt. Little spitfire. I cradled my face, looking down at the table. "I met someone."

"Oh my god!" Iphi shrieked. "That is the last thing I expected you to say. I want to hear everything. What's his name? How old is he? Where'd you meet? Oh! Or her!"

"You sound like a mom."

She jumped back. "You're right. Yuck!"

"I know you won't judge so I'll lay it out. It's not a he. Or a she. It's a them."

She cocked her head. "Them? How many are there?"

It was my turn to laugh. "Just two, it's a couple."

"Oh," Iphi clapped her hands together, "that sounds right up your alley."

Observant little imp.

"So what's the problem?" She leaned forward, focusing all her attention on me.

"Well, besides the fact that I probably can never tell my family?"

Her little face screwed up. "So first of all, it doesn't sound like your dad has been very supportive of any of your choices. Second, do you want to keep a creeper like that in your life? I mean, Burgundy," she reached out and took my hand in both of hers, "this is a man who lies, cheats on his wives, molested a good friend of yours and lets his current wife treat you like crap."

I looked away. Shit. She was right. "You make it sound so black and white."

"Because it is. Very much so. Some things just are." She shrugged. "And I suspect he's treated you like crap too, but"—a wry little smile twisted her face—"you probably chose to overlook it, make excuses or lie to yourself."

"How is it that you're so wise at nineteen?"

"It's easier to help other people navigate their problems, that's all. I'm no wiser than anyone else my age."

I squeezed her hands. "I would argue with that."

"You deserve the same thing that Sadie, Chrys and Jared have. I know you had something special with all of them, especially Sadie and Jared, and it's not that they've left you, but in a way they *have* moved on."

She was right. I was holding onto the past. The what-had-beens. With my father too. More memories of us together when I was growing up flooded back. I was little more than a toddler and he lifted me onto a horse. I was laughing with delight. When I was nine, he'd to take me into the fields with the farmers to help pick the fruit. After he became a lawyer, when I was a preteen, he took me fishing in a boat on Lago Cocibolca. I often dredged up these happy times, but I always blocked out what happened next. When that horse reared and I fell off into the dirt, my father stood over me, yelling and calling me stupid. In the fields, I overheated and he called me weak, told me that vampires didn't need water. When I begged to throw the fish back in since we didn't eat anyway, he called me a *bleeding heart*, drawing it out like a dirty word.

"I didn't raise a delicate flower, so toughen up, you idiotic girl."

And I had. I'd gotten so tough that everything, including love, had bounced right off.

"Iphi?"

"Yeah?" She let go of my hand, wearing a concerned look, and reached for her cup of tea.

"Do you think a completely unconventional relationship can work?"

"I do." She nodded. "And if anyone can make it work, you can."

Chapter Twenty-Nine

Rex and I were walking back home when my phone rang. I almost didn't answer. It was my father.

"*Hola, Papa,*" I said through gritted my teeth.

"*Hola, Maria.*" His voice was stern. "We need to talk."

"Why?"

"I have some questions for you."

"You have some questions for *me?*" My voice rose.

"What's that supposed to mean? I am still your father and I'm still the one who is paying for your house."

Nice of him to keep reminding me. Nothing's free. Carrot, meet stick. "Talk to me over the phone then."

"This needs to be in person. Meet me at my house."

"Will you be alone?"

"What does it matter? Come over now." He hung up.

My vampire heart raced uncomfortably. I didn't want to lose my father, even after everything. Even after I knew for sure that he was a prick. It would break my stoic heart. He was and always had been, emotionally, the center of my life. And I didn't want to lose my house for my friends' sakes, not mine. Where would they live? When would I see them? I wouldn't let us scatter and drift apart. I had to make this right, for them.

Might as well play the part. I dressed as conservatively as my wardrobe allowed, grabbed my keys and drove my Camaro to his house. Before I could ring the bell, my father opened the door, looking haggard. His hair was disheveled and he still wore his pajamas.

"Are you ill?" I asked, even though I knew vampires rarely got sick. Living among humans and other Signum for so long had skewed my senses a bit. He made a disgusted noise in the back of his throat and stood aside so I could enter, motioning for me to sit on the white couch just past the entryway, in their living room. Not even an offer of tea? Oh right, vampire customs.

"You look like you've put on a few extra pounds." He took the seat across from me on a chair.

"Nice to see you too."

"So why don't you tell me what you have to say for yourself, Burgundy."

"Excuse me?" I shrugged. "I like to eat."

His sigh was deep and loud. Exasperation. "I'm quite upset with you right now."

"You're. Upset. With me?" I was incredulous.

"Very." He crossed his arms over his chest. "After everything I've done for you, you betray me like this?"

"Like what?" I snapped.

"Oh, so you're going to pretend you have no idea what I'm talking about? This is how you're going to play it?"

I could only surmise that he was pissed about Amber even though he was the one who was in the wrong. Significantly so. If Amber decided to press charges I would stick by her no matter what. Even if it meant losing Casa Mañana and becoming homeless. That was the right thing to do. "I don't know what you're talking about."

He stood up and walked over to the floor-to-ceiling windows. The view was spectacular and he stood staring out at it, breathing heavily. Was he drunk?

"Let's see if I can spark your memory. You've been

saying some very nasty things about your stepmother to other people."

"What?"

"You're still going to pretend you have no idea what I'm talking about?"

"I'm not pretending. I have no idea what you're talking about."

"Deenie," my father called out loudly. "Come in here. And bring your ball."

Margery's daughter entered from the hallway, her head held so high I could see up her nose. In one hand she held her crystal ball and in the other, a stand. She set both down on the glass coffee table and looked at me with unconcealed hatred.

"You have one more chance to come clean and stop pretending, Maria," my father snarled at me.

Oh this was going to be good. "I have nothing to come clean about." I crossed my own arms over my chest.

"Deenie, show her."

The girl passed her hand over the crystal, and my meeting with Iphi that morning sparked into view. Deenie played the last part, where I told Iph what my father had done to Amber, called Margery a monster and confessed my triad.

When it was finished, she barked out a sharp laugh. "Shame on you for trying to sully your own father with lies to make my mother leave him,"

Deenie said in a high pitched voice. "You call *her* the monster?"

"Thank you, Deenie," my father said softly, "you're more of a daughter to me than my own Maria has ever been."

Wow. Stab me in the heart with a knife, why don't you? "Are you fucking kidding me? You've known this girl for what, a few months?"

"Your father practically raised me," Deenie threw back. "And he's never been anything but kind and generous to both me and my mother."

I stood up. "I think I've heard enough."

"Sit down, Maria, I am not finished," the man who called himself my father said.

I didn't sit but I didn't leave. "What more is there to say? Apparently you cheated on my mother like you cheat on Margery. Good for you, Dad. Not only are you a rapist, you're a cheater and a liar too."

"You will not speak that way to me in my house," he hissed.

Margery swept into the room, dressed in what looked like a ball gown. Weird.

"You, girl," she pointed to me, "are ungrateful. Your father has done everything for you, and this is how you repay him? It's always been about you, hasn't it, Burgundy? Conniving to see what you can get from him. Take. Take. Take. And never give. I'm not surprised to hear you call me names behind my back, but to make up such horrible lies about your own father's character. Shame on you!"

"You people are nuts." I walked to the door.

"If you walk out of that door, you'll have," he looked at his watch, "two days to come up with your mortgage, and it's no small amount either." He let out a condescending laugh. How had I never noticed that before? "And you will never be allowed back into my life."

"News flash, Dad, I don't want to be in your life. I didn't know you had such little integrity. My friends, my chosen family, have higher morals in their pinky fingers than you do in your entire body," I seethed and turned around, reaching for the doorknob.

His laugh was thick and still condescending. "Oh right, you mean like your *friends* Tiyah and Elijah?"

I spun around. "What about them?"

"They've been lying to you all along. Using you."

"Just like you use your father," spat Margery.

"What the fuck are you talking about?" If I stood there much longer I might've ripped off that woman's head.

"Your little play-toys are werewolves, you stupid girl."

Chapter Thirty

"What happened?" asked Jared the minute I walked through the door of Casa Mañana.

Instead of responding, I pulled a bounding Rex into my arms, covering his face with kisses while he tried furiously to lick mine. My little furry savior. Rex was anything but little, but I could still lift him with one hand.

I slouched down on the couch where Jared joined me and the dog sat at my feet, staring at me with pure love in his puppy-dog eyes.

"Oh god, yoga pants. Who died?"

I pushed my dark hair back over my shoulder and took a deep breath. "I was with my father. I think it's over."

"What's over?"

"My relationship with him, this house. Everything." The thought of losing Casa Mañana was almost more painful than the thought of losing my father. My friends depended on me. I had made sure of it.

"Oh, Burgundy." He gathered me up in his arms. "I'm so sorry. Is there anything I can do?"

"Besides telling Alec, Chrys and Carter that they'll soon be homeless?"

"No one's going to be homeless." His breath warmed my ear.

I wish I had his confidence about that. For years, I had been their breadwinner, their rock. They depended on me and I couldn't let them down or I would lose them. Alone, indeed.

A red tear rolled down my cheek; he wiped it away with his thumb. "We can get through this."

Alec walked in from the hallway and joined us on the couch.

Jared threw an arm around him.

"You look upset," Alec said to me.

Jared looked at me questioningly and raised one shoulder.

"You can tell him," I replied.

"It's her dad. Things aren't working out," he said to Alec.

"I'm sorry to hear that," Alec responded. "And . . . I understand how difficult dads can be sometimes."

Alec's dad was a complete ass and we all knew it.

"Dads *and* moms in my case." I laughed but it was bitter.

"Whatever we can do to help," Alec offered. "We have skills, you know."

"Oh I know." I tapped my fingers on my leg. "I need to tell you both something, but at this time, I have to swear you to secrecy."

They exchanged glances, then nodded at me.

"This is knowledge that everyone will know soon enough, but please don't spill it before the Council does."

"You have our word." Jared put his hand on my leg and I knew he was telling the truth, plus I'd always trusted him.

"Werewolves are real," I blurted.

The boys exchanged looks again before Jared barked out a laugh. "Yeah right, Burg, and pigs can fly."

I rolled my eyes at him. "So freaking cliché. Nice, Jared, but I'm serious."

He leaned forward. "How do you know?"

"Never mind the how right now."

Alec ran his fingers through his thick dark hair. "My father always said as much."

"He did?" Jared asked.

"Yeah but he never had proof to back it up, and we always thought he was just trying to scare us."

What the hell was I even thinking right now? I shouldn't have told the boys.

I stood up and started pacing in front of them. "I shouldn't have said anything. Forget it. Please."

"Why did you tell us then?" Jared asked.

"My dad's wife told me that Tiyah and Elijah are werewolves and I thought maybe you guys could shift and spy on them to find out but that is not only a ridiculously stupid idea . . . it's rude and not the kind of person I want to be."

The boys shifted in their seats.

"Spying is very uncool, yes," Alec said. "Why don't you just ask them?"

I shook my thick mane. "So many reasons." I counted them off on my finger. "I'd rather they trusted me enough to tell me. If the Council can vote them in first, I'd love to be the one to break it to them. If my stepmother weren't so vindictive and evil, I wouldn't know."

"I get it." Jared looked pained. "This can't be easy for you."

"Nothing right now is easy." Understatement of the year. But so what? Both of Jared's parents had been murdered and his sister was MIA. Sadie and Chrys's mother barely spoke to them. Alec was estranged from his father. Ryder had been an unwanted orphan. And the list went on. Everyone suffered. Tiyah and Elijah were a species of Signum that had been forced to live undercover as second-class citizens for their entire lives. Worse, they'd had to pretend to be humans. Not to minimize my strife, but really, in the scheme of things, I'd had it damn easy. I looked back at Jared and Alec, who were huddled together on the couch talking in low tones. They stood.

"We're going to our bedroom for a bit," Jared winked at me.

Spying was wrong, no matter how much I wanted to do it. There was no way I could ask my best friend for help with this. I would have to suck a fang and wait it out. When they were ready to tell me, they would. What did it matter anyway? It didn't change my feelings for them. If anything, I wanted to protect them. From my father and evil stepmother's racism, from being hurt and misunderstood, from assholes here in the Edge, shit—from assholes worldwide.

A key in the door pulled me out of my thoughts. Chrys and Carter entered, carrying a large brown bag with the logo of my favorite Italian restaurant. The scents of garlic and pesto wafted through the entire living room, commanding my attention. Carter barely ever ate human food.

"How did you know?" I followed them into the kitchen with Rex at my heels.

"Jared texted, saying you needed something to cheer you up, and we were already there getting my dinner." Chrys looked me over, then looked at Carter. "It's worse than we thought."

Stupid lounge-ware. "Can't I be comfortable in my own house?"

"Your velvet robe isn't comfortable enough?"

I didn't respond.

She piled the containers of food on the counter. "And—" She dug in the bag and brought out my absolute favorite cake. *Tres leches*.

"Oh you did not," I squealed and grabbed for it.

"She can't be that upset," teased Carter, plopping down in one of the kitchen chairs.

"What happened anyway?" Chrys asked, spooning the pasta al pesto and eggplant parmesan onto plates for us.

"Lover drama. Family drama. Drama drama." I sat down next to Chrys to help distribute the goodies.

She shook her head. "Stupid families. Who needs 'em?"

I spooned a giant helping of food into my mouth to avoid blurting, "I do!"

"If it were only that easy, right?" Carter laughed, then glanced at me. "Hey, slow down there, speedy. Don't you want to savor it?"

"I am," I responded around a mouthful of bread.

We were finishing up dinner when Alec appeared in the kitchen doorway, hair disheveled and wearing a big grin.

"I know what you've been up to." I winked at him. His grin broadened. "Hungry?"

"Definitely." He joined us at the kitchen table.

"Jared?" I enquired.

"Sleeping. I wore him out." Alec helped himself to a plate.

After he finished eating, Alec padded back to his room but he was only gone a few minutes before popping back into the kitchen, looking worried.

"Did any of you see Jared?" he asked.

We looked at one another and all shook our heads.

"What's wrong?"

"He's gone and the window's open."

"Gone? Where would he go?" asked Chrys.

Alec's lips had thinned and he was shaking his head at me. Shit. Had he left to spy on my lovers? No way. What reason would he have to do that? Plus I'd told him how I felt about spying and he'd agreed. Hadn't he?

"What should we do?" I asked.

"I'm shifting and looking for him."

"Please don't. You don't know where he is. Let me call Elijah and see if he's there."

"And say what? My bestie may be spying on you without my consent to see if you're—."

"Shhh," I hissed.

Carter and Chrys exchanged looks.

"I'm going to track him," Alec huffed. "Please don't try and stop me."

I followed Alec into their bedroom, holding up my hands. "I won't try to stop you. I want to come with you."

"No way, you'll just slow me down. Hold tight and I'll be back with Jared as soon as I find him."

He disappeared into their walk-in closet, skittering out moments later in his spider-monkey form. Before I could do or say anything, he leapt out of their already-open window. I closed it behind him.

I changed out of the loungeware, waved goodbye to Chrys and Carter on their way to Chrys's bedroom and grabbed Rex. Then I hurried to my car, intending to drive around our quaint town and take my mind off things. But ten minutes later, without thinking, I was parking in the houseboat lot. Had my pussy led me here, or my heart? I did not want to do a drop-by without asking and picked up my phone. But just as I was about to text my couple, there was a ping. Were they on the same wavelength as me?

Apparently not.

It was from a blocked number and read, *Found your spy*.

What the hell? A replay of the Jared and Alec abduction from last summer flashed through my mind.

Another text came in. It was a photo of Jared in his fox form, trapped in a tiny cage. I gnashed my fangs.

Instinct had led me to the docks after all.

Chapter Thirty-One

Ryder's witchy family lived on a boat at the end of Gate Three. The Gates were part of the houseboat community, and while some of them had been renovated over the years, Gate Three stood in disrepair.

The others had been rebuilt above the water with thick railings. They boasted artwork and potted flowers along the pathways, but not this one. It was the last gate still floating haphazardly on the water's surface. There were no railings or handholds, and Gate Three had garnered more than a few tales about drunks falling off the sides late at night.

I walked carefully down the dock, which pitched and leaned as the ocean swelled. The wooden slats were splintered and uneven, but my lightning-quick reflexes stopped me from tumbling into the water.

Rex ran ahead of me, off leash. It was easier than navigating with him as well. By the time I reached Ryder's mom's house, I was having second thoughts. Should I have gone back home instead to burst in on Chrys and Carter's lovemaking, begging for her help? Totally disrespectful and a waste of precious minutes. No. I pounded on the door and Katharine appeared in her bathrobe, holding a cup of coffee. The woman and her daughter were of Native American descent. Their long, dark hair, skin the color of sand and high cheekbones rivaled the world's most renowned models.

"Burgundy," she said. "What's wrong?"

"Can I come inside?"

"Of course. And you brought Rex." She bent down and pet the pooch, then stepped aside for us to enter.

Katharine's house changed often, especially the interior, as she loved to cast decorating and redecorating spells. This time it was all art deco and it looked fantastic. Originally I had thought that decorating spells and other surface-level manipulations were a type of glamour, but it turned out that some witches could physically shape items too. Katharine fell into the latter category, an enviable trait for anyone who loved to be surrounded by an ever-changing personal landscape.

Following her onto their houseboat, I explained

the situation while she brought me a cup of coffee in a sci-fi-looking metal cup.

As we settled on the couch, another text came in. *Your proof: ask a question only he would know the answer to.* That would mean he'd shifted back. Katharine went to get her crystal ball. There was so much to pick from that only Jared would know, but most of it was confidential. There was a knock on the door and I leapt out of my seat.

"Can you get that, Burgundy?" Katharine called from the other end of the house.

"Sure." I crossed to the threshold. "Who it is?" I asked.

"It's me," Alec sounded distraught. I threw open the door.

"How'd you know where I was?"

He pointed to his nose. "And your car in the lot . . ." He was visibly shaking and I put my arm around him protectively.

"What happened?" I asked him.

"Jared's scent disappears on Elijah's boat."

"Are you sure?" So they had him?

"I'm sure." His entire body was convulsing.

Why on earth would my couple kidnap my best friend? There was absolutely no reason to.

Alec pulled away, holding up his hands. "What?"

I handed him my phone and he read the texts, his mouth unhinged, nostrils flaring.

"I will fucking kill them," he growled in a low voice and then punched something in. I read over his shoulder. *What were we searching for in China last summer? Spelled in Chinese pinyin.*

Katharine returned moments later with her ball, candles and her athame. "Alec, welcome, I'm glad you're here. We'll find Jared."

"Katharine," he hugged her, "I hope so."

The phone beeped again and Alec looked at it while I peered over his shoulder.

Zhūshā

"Someone fucking has him." Alec handed the phone back to me. The sides of his jaw bulged from gnashing his teeth.

Katharine tapped her crystal ball when the next text came in. *We will text you our demands.* I slammed the phone down.

"I feel completely helpless," Alec growled.

"Katherine's going to try and find him, okay?"

Alec nodded, but instead of sitting, he paced in front of the couch while Ryder's mom cast a circle around her crystal ball.

"Show us Jared." She passed her hand over it but it remained blank.

We both looked at her quizzically.

"Strange," she said. "It should work." She removed a pendulum from a carved wooden box on her coffee table. "Is the crystal being blocked?"

The pendulum rotated in a wide circle, indicating the answer was yes.

"By another witch?" Nothing. She put the pendulum down, sighing. "It's impossible." She rubbed her forehead. "I wish there was something else I could do."

"As soon as I'm able to shift back, I will," Alec barked, eyes narrowing.

"What can you do if you don't know where he is?" I asked.

He ran his fingers through his dark hair, mussing it. The poor man looked like he was going to explode. I desperately wanted to protect him. And Jared. They were *my* responsibility. This was all happening because of me. I sure was a shitty friend.

"Why isn't your ball working?" Alec asked.

"There are a few explanations I can think of. Either another shifter masked his scent or another witch cast a spell ." She tossed her long brown hair.

"Why the hell would anyone do that?" asked Alec.

"No idea," she huffed. "Unfortunately, not all Signum use their powers with integrity."

That was the understatement of the year.

Alec took a step toward the front door. "The longer we stay here talking, the more danger Jared is in. Do you remember what happened last time? With Landry and the trackers?"

How could I forget? Both Jared and Alec had

been captured and tortured. It had been particularly bad for Jared, though, since his sister had been involved.

"I'm the one responsible for this mess. I need to find him and I may know where he is." I white-knuckled Katharine's couch.

Alec dug his fingernails into his palm. "We go together."

"Of course, but first I have to be sure." There was no way I wanted Alec to know who I suspected, especially if it was true.

Chapter Thirty-Two

I dropped Alec off at home, making him promise to wait there while I checked out a lead. He was reticent to let me out of his sight, and normally I would have just insisted. It was my inherent Dominatrix. But this time I pleaded instead, which may be why he acquiesced.

"One hour," he hissed at me as I left the house.

Sitting in my carport below the house, with Cherry's engine already running, I called my lovers.

"Jah," answered Tiyah's sweet voice, pinging my heart. I'd never believe she could kidnap Jared, but Jonas? He was a wild card. How far would he go to protect his pack?

Be cool, be breezy. "Where you guys at?"

"The shop, getting ready for a dive. Wanna join us?"

"I'll be right there."

Less than five minutes later, I walked into The Barnacle and straight into Tiyah's arms, placing a kiss on her warm cheek.

Jonas froze in the midst of stepping into a wet suit. "What the hell is she doing here?"

"And a cheerful hello to you," I responded.

"Jonas, please, Burgundy is our friend." Tiyah took one look at my face and steered me into the back office.

"With friends like that . . ." he grumbled in our wake.

"What's up?" she asked once we were alone.

"Someone's kidnapped Jared." I searched for a tell. Jonas had looked grumpy, but not hostile. But he could have been faking it, and I didn't know him well enough to tell. But there was no way in hell Tiyah could hide anything from her Domme.

"What?" Her eyes widened. "Oh my god. Why?"

"I don't know. I don't know who has him *or* why they took him."

"What can we do?"

I lowered my voice. "You don't think Jonas would do anything like that, do you?"

She barked out a laugh. "No way. Why would you even ask that?"

"Because he hates me." *And because Jared went to spy on you*, I didn't add.

"That doesn't mean he'd do something dangerous and illegal. I'm offended you'd even think that."

"I'm sorry." I palmed my eyes, dropping into the office chair. I'd gotten Jared into this mess but how would I get him out? "I don't know what to think."

Tiyah was at my side, crouching next to me, hugging me close. "Shhh, it'll be okay." She pet my hair and kissed my cheek. I turned my head and our lips met. It wasn't a kiss of lust or desire. The touch of her mouth on mine was yielding, offering comfort, as her arms circled me.

"What the hell?"

Tiyah jumped away.

Jonas stood in the doorway, hands on his hips, eyes locked on Tiyah. "Shit, I knew something fishy was going on, but I didn't peg *you* as the cheater." His eyes narrowed, nostrils flaring. "How dare you."

Elijah rushed in, a wet suit over his shoulder. "What's going on?"

"Turns out your wife is a dyke." His eyes flashed.

Oh for fuck's sake.

I held Tiyah in my arms, stroking her curls while we waited for Elijah in my car. He had stayed behind in the dive shop to try and calm down his brother.

"Well, I guess that cat's out of the bag."

"Yeah," her voice hiccupped.

"Do you think he'll be okay with it?"

She shook her head. "He's really old-fashioned. I don't know."

"He wants the best for his brother and for you. No?" I twisted around to meet her gaze.

She nodded, then winced. "It's not that simple."

"Nothing ever is."

My phone vibrated and I dug it out of my purse.

Cut your father out of your life. Tell him you hate him and want nothing more to do with him and your friend will be released unharmed.

I rolled my eyes and showed the text to Tiyah, who shook her head. "What?"

"Well at least I know who has him now." And this would be the last time I underestimated the depths to which they'd stoop.

The back passenger door opened and Elijah slid in behind his wife.

"Jonas will come around. Eventually." He leaned between the seats. "So what's the plan?"

Instead of starting the car, I swiveled my body around. "I need your help. It looks like my evil step-monster has Jared."

"What can we do?" Elijah asked.

The uncomfortable moment of truth. I took a

deep breath and held it while they both looked at me expectantly. "I know what you are," I blurted.

The couple exchanged looks, and then Tiyah said, "What we are?"

Fuck, here goes. "I know you're both werewolves."

After a stunned silence, Elijah growled, "How the hell did you find out?"

"Margery told me but I didn't believe her." I winced. Better to get it all out in the open if I hoped for a future with them. "I confided in Jared and I'm guessing he thought he owed me something, which prompted him to spy on you."

"Are you fucking kidding?" said Elijah. "You sent someone to spy on us?"

Tiyah's eyes filled with tears.

I turned to look pleadingly to look at Elijah. "I didn't send him but I do take personal responsibility. He obviously thought that's what I wanted."

He shook his head, his eyes flashing with anger.

"And when he was kidnapped, I thought Jonas had taken him," I blurted in a rush to get it all out.

Tiyah let out a gasp and Elijah opened the passenger door, muttering "Un-fucking-believeable".

"Wait." I put my hand on her arm. "Please. I'm sorry. With everything that's happened, my head isn't in the right place."

"So what? You suddenly lost your ability to communicate? You go to Jared first about the secret we have to keep in order to survive, instead of coming to us? Something you say convinces him that spying is a good idea. And then, if that weren't enough, you suspect my own brother of doing something illegal and immoral? Burgundy, how can we trust you now?" Elijah put a foot on the ground and swiveled, but Tiyah held up a hand.

"Please, honey." Her tone was soft, soothing. "Let's get Jared back safely and then we'll discuss this."

Chapter Thirty-Three

The sun was setting as we drove in heated silence to my dad's house. I'd texted Alec, who said he'd meet us there after he shifted. The front porch lights blazed and I rang the bell, posing with my hands on my hips and the evilest eye I could muster.

Turns out, werewolves were expert scent trackers. The plan was for Elijah and Tiyah to find Jared while I distracted the witch. And if Alec was there to help them, all the better.

After five minutes of me ringing the bell—the last minute, continuously—Margery finally opened the door. "Burgundy, what an unexpected surprise. Your father isn't here right now."

"That's okay, Margery, I wanted to talk to you."

"I wish I could, dear, but now isn't good for me."

She took a step outside, closing the door behind her. "Let's figure out another time."

"Let me ask you something before I leave."

Her mouth popped open even as her eyes narrowed. "Yes?"

"Why did you marry my dad?"

"Because we're in love," she answered like I was a moron.

"The truth, please. If I'm going to give you what you want and disappear from his life, don't I deserve to know?"

A sly smile spread across her plastic Barbie mouth. "Okay." She leaned against the doorjamb. "You know, you are the complete opposite of your mother. Good for you, standing up for yourself."

Jesus, this woman charged by the hour—did she pad her billables with this obsequious fluff?

She took a breath, then huffed. "Besides the fact that your father and I complement each other in so many ways—"

I arched a brow.

"—his prestige and financial security will secure a place for me and my daughter."

It was that base? "You're a lawyer as well. Surely you have plenty of your own money. You told me so yourself."

"A couple million compared to your father's billions is nothing. I became a lawyer late in life, quite late, and I'm tired of working. This way Deenie will be able to go to any school she wants and pursue a career of her choice. I can quit working and travel the world. It opens every door."

"My father can just divorce you and you'll lose everything. Especially if he finds out you only married him for his money."

Her laughter rang out in a cackle worthy of a Disney villainess. "Your father married a divorce lawyer, dear. You don't think I knew what to do so he can never leave me? He'd lose everything, I made sure of that."

I snarled, lunging for the woman's face. If I tore her repugnant lashes out, would Dad still want her?

Deenie shrieked, and from the corner of my eye, I saw her draw a symbol in the air. My hands stopped a mere inch from her mother's face as if they'd hit a pane of glass. Turning to look at her daughter, I caught fading wisps of smoke disintegrating.

A loud crash and the sound of breaking glass came from downstairs.

"Girl," her mother snarled, "leave her."

M argery threw the front door open and took a step inside, but I yanked her back, spun her around and shoved her a solid ten feet down the elaborate flagstone entryway. She didn't teeter on her four-inch Louboutins—the bitch was nearly as solid in them as I was—but a race between a pissed-off vamp and a pearl-clutching cliché of a trophy wife? No contest.

I rushed through the doorway, then slammed and locked the door in her face. The thump of her body flying into the ten-foot oak monstrosity was oh so gratifying.

I dashed toward the sounds of a commotion, down a set of stairs and into a long hallway flanked by multiple doors. But I didn't have to time to pause and check each one. A loud growl drew me to a door at the end of the hallway, and in a split second, I was inside.

A thousand-pound brown bear stood over a cat carrier with a red fox inside. Elijah and Tiyah were crouched together in the opposite corner, trying to look as non-threatening as possible. But Alec took a step toward them anyway, one giant paw raised.

"Alec, no!" I cried out.

His head whipped in my direction. I pointed to the broken glass sliding door. "Go!" To my shock, he actually listened. He leapt through the window, clutching the cage to his chest, as someone—two someones?—barreled down the hallway behind me.

I whipped around to face whoever it was, then did a double take at what passed the threshold. At first glance, it looked like Margery and her daughter, but their facades wavered, as if the air between us was simmering with ferocious heat. A loud pop echoed around us. The silver-haired twins distorted, their faces melting from the ones I knew into something entirely different. Something ghastly. Both mouths gaped open in a scene worthy of Edvard Munch. Something crunched behind me, and I spun around. My lovers stood, ready to pounce on the witches, to protect me, but there was fear in Tiyah's eyes. For me or them?

"I've got this," I mouthed to them. Then I jutted my chin toward the gaping window.

They turned and fled through the broken sliding glass door.

Chapter Thirty-Four

With everyone I loved safely out of the line of fire, I heaved a quick breath of relief. I spun around, facing the witches whose facades were back in place. An illusion? A hallucination? A seriously delayed acid trip from my younger years?

Margery folded her hands over her chest while Deenie glared at me.

"Does my father know you kidnapped my best friend?"

She shook her head, the white bob sashaying with the movement.

"So why'd you do it?"

"He's the one who came to us. Caught him sniffing around outside. Didn't know what he was up against."

"You could have ignored him or shooed him away. But you didn't."

"Ah, yes, well, that's not my style. Someone comes sniffing around me and my daughter," she narrowed her eyes, "I show them who's boss."

Deenie beamed, blinking her own mascara-clad eyes like a younger clone of her mother.

"But you're not asking *that*, are you, dear? You're asking why I imprisoned your friend, correct?"

I crossed my hands over my chest.

"To show you where the game really stands. If you don't leave your father to me and sever contact with him forever, I'll make sure that all of your little friends suffer. And I don't mean they'll be caged. I mean, they'll be dead."

I had no intention of finding out if this woman was bluffing. Had I wanted a relationship with my father—if he'd treated me with kindness and respect —her threats would not have stopped me. But seeing as he was blinded by this beast and had already chosen her over me, I wasn't interested in pursuing anything with him.

"All of this just for my father's money. Seems too superficial, even for you."

The hag's lips curved up into a grimace I suspected was a smile. "Money *and* power. Deenie and I will be set for our very long life, and with you out of the picture, your father won't be torn between," she air quoted, " 'loyalties.' "

"And?" I said, waiting.

"And?" She tossed her hair.

"Admit it, Margery, you did all of this just to see if you could pull it off. It gives your measly existence a jolt of superiority so you can pretend you're better than."

She coughed out a laugh. "I don't have to pretend. I *am* better than you. But, I'll concede, I do love the challenge. The chase. The game. I love bringing you to your knees—figuratively, of course."

"You're really sick."

"What's this?" My father entered the room, looking between the three of us and then at the broken glass. "Maria, what have you done now?"

A bark of laughter erupted from me. "What have *I* done? When you wake up from your midlife crisis in a few years, Dad, remember this. Remember that it was your choice to treat your only daughter like a piece of shit and push her out of your life. Your choice to completely abandon your wife and children. Your choice to marry a monster."

His face reddened and he lunged for me, but I sidestepped him and he grasped air. I knew him too well.

"When that day comes, don't bother trying to

claw your way back to your real family because we won't be here for you anymore. That bridge has been burned to ashes, and you're the one who lit the match. " With my uncanny speed, I disappeared through the broken window, not bothering to look back.

Chapter Thirty-Five

Tiyah and Elijah weren't answering their phones. I debated showing up at their boat but I wanted them to have time to cool off, time for Tiyah to bring her husband around. Instead, I texted Alec and Jared.

Where are you two? Are you OK?

Alec pinged back. *We're safe, at Casa Mañana. Tucked Jared into bed. You?*

I stopped at Sadie's. Why did Jared get end up at Margery's in the first place?

He felt obligated to help. You know him. He didn't want you to lose your house.

Shit, it really was my fault that his life had been in danger. Of course he felt obligated. It was his way of "paying me back." When had our friendship become so inauthentic, so filled with give and take?

Talk later? I'm going to snuggle my boyfriend now, Alec texted.

Sure, give him a kiss for me, I responded, putting my phone down on Sadie's coffee table.

Ryder brought me a second cup of hot cocoa, then plopped down on the couch next to his fiancée while she cradled me on her other side. I spent thirty minutes confiding in them, telling them everything from the existence of werewolves to the spell my stepsister had cast on me.

"I'm so sorry you had to deal with that. And poor Jared. What was he thinking?" Sadie said.

I flinched. "I think he felt obligated to help."

"He has been expressing a lot of guilt about living there rent-free with Alec. It's tearing him up." Her voice was firm.

I needed to make all of this right somehow. "Jared's not beholden to me for helping him. I don't know exactly when our friendship became so skewed."

"When Alec moved in, I think. Jared's been feeling subpar. Not only can't he fully support himself, but he can't support his man either. It emasculates a guy."

"He's in school full-time. When he becomes a chiropractor, he'll likely make much more money than I do. Why can't he help out then?"

"Because you've been helping him since he was

eighteen, Burgundy. That's years of not being able to carry his own weight, and now he's doubled the load. You know how independent he is."

I did. Had I been supporting him all of these years so he'd be dependent on me and never able to leave me? Or had I done it as a carrot to dangle in front of him, just like my father did to me? Or the most pathetic reason of all—had I done it so that he would love me because without money I wasn't worthy?

"Hey." Sadie put her hand on my shoulder. "Whatever's going on in your head right now is probably wrong. Jared loves you for who you are, not for what you've provided. That's why he went out of his way for you today."

"Great, that doesn't help. I feel so guilty and angry—with myself."

"Not productive." Sadie got up and went into the other room while Ryder rubbed my back. She returned moments later with a large book.

She placed the ancient-looking tome on her living-room table and opened it up. A musky scent invaded my nostrils, making me sneeze.

Sadie flipped through several pages and I caught the title of one chapter: *Blood Lines*. She stopped on a page depicting two women who looked exactly like Margery and her daughter. Straight, stark-white hair and large, dark eyes. Their iridescent skin looked inhuman. Next to them were symbols drawn in smoke. Sadie tapped the page, which read, *Ordo Hermeticus Aurorae Aureae* (*Order of the Golden Dawn*).

"But . . . how did you know?"

"I didn't. I vaguely remembered this picture from leafing through the book when I was a little girl, with Aurelia."

All three of us leaned closer to the book.

"Is it black magic?" I asked.

She shook her head. "All magic can be used for good or bad. White or black. Depends on the practitioner."

We all returned our gaze to the volume, reading in silence.

I pointed. "It says that the belief system of these witches is self-serving. They believe you can live as gods on Earth."

Ryder nodded. "That makes sense. Our belief is the opposite." He gestured between Sadie and himself. "We glorify nature. Both our families spring from the same lineage, Neo-Paganism."

Sadie continued, "We respect the Earth and the heavens. Margery's practice puts themselves first, even above other humans and Signum."

"So basically the Order of the Golden Dawn is a cult of narcissists?" I asked.

"Looks that way." Sadie pulled a face.

"Great, so I'd call that evil." How could it be labeled as anything else?

Sadie shook her head. "Not evil. Self-serving."

"There's a difference?" I asked.

"They're not Satanists." Ryder tapped the page. "They don't kill people, mutilate or destroy. They bend and manipulate reality for their own personal gain."

"So this is really why they want me out of the picture, not part of my father's life."

"Removing the only foreseen obstacle. That does make sense," Sadie said.

"They're planning to use his power and prestige for personal gain," Ryder added.

Hadn't Margery confirmed exactly that?

Sadie picked up the book, studying it closer, turning a page and reading some more before she let out a long breath. "It says here that werewolves are their kryptonite."

"Well that explains her vehemence, why she doesn't want them in the Edge. But why do they fear werewolves so much?"

"Apparently, werewolves hunt and destroy their kind and other offshoot orders because they're 'destroyers of the light.' "

I tsked. "That's certainly colorful. But what the heck does it mean?"

"Not a clue. But I know who you can ask."

Chapter Thirty-Six

The next morning I parked in front of city hall and sat waiting in the lobby. Picking my cuticles passed the time as the Council met behind closed doors.

When the door to the meeting room door finally opened, it was flung with so much force that it slammed into the opposite wall. My dad stomped out, his voice deep and angry. "The vote was rigged."

Benedict hurried out after him. "Mr. Rosales, wait. What are you talking about?"

"There's a werewolf on the Council, disguised as a shifter," he snarled. "Are you going to pretend you didn't know?"

I jumped to my feet, freezing in plain view. Holding my chin high, I kept my eyes trained on Benedict. My breath grew shallow as I willed my legs to take root. Let my father see me. Even though it hurt like hell, I didn't have to show it. I wanted him to believe that I couldn't care less about him. Mask firmly in place. A seamless façade.

"No, Mr. Rosales. To whom are you referring?"

Other Council members flowed out of the room, only to stop in their tracks at my father's ugly expression. Worried eyes darted around.

"Him." My father pointed at Jonas, who had filed out with the others. "He's a damn werewolf."

Benedict turned to him. "Is this true?"

People gasped and the woman closest to him retreated back into the room.

"Yes, sir," he responded loudly, his chest puffed out, eyes locked on my father.

"Would you like to explain yourself?" Benedict's voice was composed.

"How is it fair to vote on our race without having one of us present?"

My father stiffened, flashing his fangs.

Benedict held a hand up. "Hervé, can you take the others back inside? I'll be in presently."

"Without him?" My father's eyes were wild.

"Yes, for a revote."

Grumbling under his breath, my dad and the others returned to the meeting room.

He hadn't even bothered to acknowledge my presence. Good.

Benedict turned to Jonas. "I understand your position but I'm afraid that's not how things are done here. We have to vote again without you. You can wait here for the outcome, but I'd advise you to leave. For your own safety."

Jonas bowed his head.

"I'll call you as soon as the meeting adjourns." Benedict disappeared back inside, closing the door behind him.

At the audible click, Jonas faced me. Guess my housefly impression needed work. "Why are you here?"

"I was hoping to talk to you."

"Me? Why? I need to get out of here and warn my brother. If things go south in there—"

"This isn't the 1800s, no one's going to run you out of town."

"I wouldn't be so sure. People fear what they don't understand and the response to fear is usually aggression. Violence."

"Call Elijah, but then . . . give me five minutes, that's all I'm asking you for."

Sitting at an outside table at a cafe across the street from city hall, I sipped iced tea and waited for Jonas.

As he stood on the sidewalk talking on his cell phone to Elijah, gesturing animatedly, I couldn't help but note their similarities. There was much I didn't know about this breed of Signum, but I wanted to learn. Not just because they fascinated me, but because two of their people had lassoed my heart, cinching it up tightly.

His call apparently at an end, Jonas stowed the phone in his pocket, made his way across the patio and took the chair opposite me.

"Thank you for agreeing to have coffee with me," I said.

"I'm doing it for my brother." The waiter approached, but Jonas waved him away.

"That's one thing I want to talk to you about. Our relationship—"

"He tried to explain it to me, they both have. It's the only reason I'm sitting here with you right now."

"Can we table it for a moment? There's something else I want to discuss with you."

"No, we cannot." He cocked his thick brows at me. He was not making this easy.

I took a deep breath, pushing my hair out of my face. I'd keep this simple. "I don't know what they've told you, but I'm in love with them. Both of them." Damn it felt good to say that aloud. Elijah may be upset with me now, but we'd work it out, even if I had to grovel. I needed them.

Jonas shook his head.

"I'm not asking you to understand, but for their sake, I hope that you'll try to accept it. Me. Us." I made an encompassing gesture with my hands. "Obviously it's not your typical relationship, but for the three of us, it works. And I know you want to see your brother and Tiyah happy. I," I put my hand flat on my chest, "make them happy. And vice versa."

"With your"—he gestured to my ample chest—" attributes?"

If his lip weren't curled up in one corner, just the tiniest bit, I would have stormed off. Instead, I steepled my fingers in front of my large bosom, drawing his attention there while keeping my violet eyes steely. He sighed, shaking his head and forced his gaze back up to mine.

"You're right, I don't get it. I get the idea of some fun and exploration. Hell, what man doesn't fantasize about being serviced by two women?" He took a sip of water, licking his lips. "I understand the difference between sex and emotional attachment. I don't like to separate them myself, I'm old-fashioned in that way, but I do understand it. What you're proposing is a complete contrast to what I believe a relationship should be, and I just can't wrap my head around it."

You and most everyone else in this world. "I get that it's not conventional, but will you try? I'm not asking for you to introduce me as their wife. I'm asking for you to acknowledge the love we have for each other. To look past the conventions of society and focus instead on the ways that our triad does work."

Jonas signaled to the waiter, ordering coffee for us before turning his attention back to me. He leaned back in his chair. "Obviously you accept our species, and for that I'm grateful. So for that reason and for my pack, I'll try."

I clapped my hands together.

"But I can't promise anything. Clear?"

"Crystal."

The waiter placed two steaming mugs in front of us and Jonas nodded in return. Leaning his elbows on the table, he cradled his cup. "All right, I'm ready for the next order of business."

I took a sip of my own coffee, then cleared my throat. "The Order of the Golden Dawn."

His lip curled into a snarl. "Don't tell me those assholes have settled in the Edge too."

"I'd never heard of them before yesterday."

"But today?"

"My stepmother. The woman my father married and her daughter."

He slammed a fist down on the table. "That's why your father doesn't want us here."

"But my father doesn't know what they are," I interjected. "She's influencing him, using him. He has no clue why."

"Your father is not a stupid man."

"Stupid? No. Weak and easily controlled? Yes." Wow, that felt good to admit.

"Are you telling me because you need information about them, or are you telling me in order to warn me?"

"Both. I want to know what they are and why they're so afraid of your kind, but as I've already proved, I care about your pack and I want to make sure you're all safe."

His hard features softened, just a little. "Thank you." He sipped his coffee. "And does Elijah know they're here? The Dawn?"

"I think he does now. Both him and Tiyah got up close and personal with them yesterday. I saw . . . I don't know what I saw. It was like they just *changed* when Tiyah and Elijah got near them. Is that why the Dawn fears you?"

"They can't hold their glamours or cast spells when we're around. We act as a true mirror."

"Is that why they call you 'destroyers of the light'?"

He roared. "Nice, dramatic name for a mirror, right? They call us that so others will fear us. They want people to think we really do bring darkness, but it's the opposite. We dispel illusion."

"And that's why you've been in hiding forever."

"It's one reason. It's why most still wish to remain hidden, those that are left, anyway."

I cocked my head.

"Witches from the Order of the Golden Dawn have been hunting us for millennia."

"How come no other witches know of your existence either? Surely they could find you in their crystal balls."

"One of our other gifts. Our race had to adapt, to evolve in order to remain alive." He sat back, a smug smile splitting those ruddy cheeks. "We're invisible to scrying."

I didn't want to ask him to put in a good word for me, but I was on the outs with my lovers, unable to reach them. "Jonas?"

He cocked his head just like a predator, listening for their prey. "Can you tell Elijah that we had this talk and that I'm sorry?"

"For what?" His nostrils flared.

"I'd rather not say. It was an incorrect presumption on my part as well as some hurtful actions and I've learned from my mistakes."

His eyes softened. "Everyone deserves a second chance. I'll see what I can do."

Chapter Thirty-Seven

Tiyah and Elijah still weren't accepting my phone calls or responding to my texts. When Eli had asked to pick up the discussion later, I didn't think he meant in the next lifetime, so I did what any lovestruck woman would do. I showed up at their boat, which was berthed at the end of Trinidad Marina. I paused on the dock out front, anxious.

The sailboat looked bigger than I'd expected from Alec and Jared's descriptions, but I had little boating experience. I had imagined the living quarters jutting out above the water, but they were nestled down below with small portholes and a wooden door at the stern.

I stepped aboard to ring the heavy brass bell that hung outside.

A shade next to the porthole window flipped up,

but before I could see a face, it swished back into place.

"Go away," Elijah's voice rang out.

"Please. We need to talk."

Clipped laughter. "That's ripe. Now you need to talk?"

"Give me five minutes."

"Why?"

"Because you agreed to talk to me after Jared was free, and it's been *days*."

I stopped, strangling back the hurt and abandonment. I wasn't going to take out my feelings on my friends anymore. And I wasn't going to cajole, shame or manipulate them into doing what I wanted. I wasn't going to stoop to my father's ways, not ever again.

I started over, composed this time. "I will not just let you both go, not without a face-to-face. I'm all in, guys. As crazy as it sounds, I'm one hundred percent committed to our relationship. If you don't want it to end, than we need to be able to discuss issues when someone's feelings get hurt."

Silence.

I'd tried. I wouldn't force it. "When you're ready, let me know. Until then, you know where to find me but know I still consider us an item." I turned around and walked back down their finger dock. But before I got to the next berth, the heavy lock disengaged and the door creaked open.

"Burgundy, wait." It was Tiyah. I swiveled around and took in her stark figure poised in the doorway. "Come inside." She disappeared and I followed.

Despite my anxiety over our future, I couldn't help gasping at the interior. Dark wood lined everything—the walls, the floor, the center kitchen. Gorgeous. One wall housed a wraparound leather couch with a wood table in the center, and the opposite wall sported a matching leather loveseat with a wooden side table.

"I'm not going to offer you anything to drink," Tiyah said, snapping me out of admiring the marble-topped bar in the corner. I hadn't been angling for a cocktail. Though some liquid courage would've really helped right about then.

She slid into the booth and I sat across from her.

"Can I talk to both of you? Please."

"Elijah's still holding a grudge."

This had to about more than just not confronting them about being werewolves. "I want to apologize to him, to both of you." I propped my elbows on the table. "I should have asked you first, as soon as Margery said it."

"Why didn't you?" Tiyah blinked her long lashes at me.

And that was the million-dollar question right now, wasn't it. "I guess I was afraid."

Tiyah snorted. "That it was true."

"No," I held up my hands, "that's not what I meant."

Elijah appeared from the back, phone in hand, shaking his head. "How you won over my brother I have no idea, but for that I'll hear you out." He slid in next to his wife.

My hands worried themselves, betraying my nerves. But he was here, willing to listen. Warm relief coursed through my veins.

"I'm sorry. I screwed up and I wanted to apologize to you both—in person."

"Go on." He leaned back, crossing his arms over his broad pecs.

Tiyah's eyes blazed but she said nothing.

Would they let me in or cut me off for good? If they'd hear me out, maybe I could rectify the situation. I leaned forward in the cramped space and looked from one to the other. "I should have talked to you both in person as soon as I found out what you were and not spilled secrets that weren't mine to tell. If I had done that, Jared would not have tried to spy on you or been kidnapped. I take full responsibility for that. And I acknowledge that it was ridiculous of me to suspect Jonas. Now that I know him a little better, I'm embarrassed that I thought he had anything to do with it. Hell, I'm embarrassed about how I dealt with this entire situation."

They exchanged glances.

"Thank you for acknowledging that." Tiyah's lips curved and my heart sped up.

Elijah ran his hands through his hair. "One thing that we advocate and have worked hard to achieve in our own relationship is taking personal responsibility for our actions. I'm glad to see you came to that on your own."

"Well I do have my father to thank for that. Finger-pointing is a defensive move and unfair fighting." I leaned back, the tension in my body flowing out.

"Good," Tiyah slowly grinned at me, "we're on the same page. So why did you ask us to get involved with Jared's capture? Alec had it covered."

"Because I wasn't sure if he could handle it. He was in reaction mode, and as we all know," I splayed my hands, "when acting from emotions, things don't usually go well."

They both nodded at me.

"I had no idea what we'd find there or if Alec and I could handle it on our own."

My lovers exchanged looks.

"That was the right answer," said Elijah, "even if it was the wrong execution."

"We want you to come to us for help. And vice versa," said Tiyah.

"Like all people in new relationships, we have kinks to work out." Elijah cocked his head and held up a hand. "Pun intended. No comments from the peanut gallery, please." He motioned for all of us to stand.

We did and he threw his arms around me and his wife, pulling us both into a bear hug.

Chapter Thirty-Eight

The entire town was on edge. It was the first full moon since we'd been told werewolves existed. The Council was strongly leaning toward a yes vote but wanted to see what would happen during a full moon first.

Jonas had assured them that they'd been in the Edge during prior full moons, but that hadn't been enough.

"What do you do?" I was standing on my lovers' boat, looking out at the water as sunshine sparked and glimmered off the surface and the fish undulated just beneath.

"When we change, you mean?" asked Tiyah. She lounged on the deck in a skimpy bathing suit. I was grateful for the uncharacteristic October heat wave.

"Yeah, tonight, during the full moon. How do you keep from . . ." I trailed off, realizing too late just how offensive I was sounding.

"Killing people?" she finished. She mimed swiping at me with her nonexistent claws. The playful smile on her face let me off the hook.

I stuck my tongue out at her, though inside I reminded myself to stop playing tourist. But there was no easy way to ask these questions. If I was having trouble asking my lovers these questions, how had Benedict done it? I could only imagine the exchange behind those closed doors. Locked in a room with Jonas for an hour as the alpha persuaded the Council's chair that werewolves were merely overgrown puppies? Woof.

I waited, not wanting to appear nervous or eager.

"Why do you think we live on this boat?" she said.

Oh. "You take her out and change in the middle of the ocean?"

"We do," Elijah answered for her, walking toward us in dark-gray cutoffs. "Our pack gathers here; there are five of us. We anchor her out and keep to ourselves."

"Can't you swim?"

"No. Well, that's not exactly true. We can swim short distances, and if we smell food or blood . . ."

Tiyah shrugged. "Look, we can't apologize for who we are any more than you can."

"I'm not judging." I held up both hands. "I'm curious. I love Jared and Alec in all their forms." I was sure I'd love these two as well.

"We have it under control. There are plenty of our kind who don't but most of us do. Being hunted is the worst and our race is smaller than any of the others." Elijah dropped to his knees next to Tiyah, kissing her bare shoulder.

"I feel so close to you both. You're my chosen partners but this feels like such a huge rift. I don't know what happens, or what you do. It's like a part of your life that's secret and if I don't know all of you—how can I love all of you?"

"Nice try." Elijah smiled up at me. "Come here." He patted the area next to him and I sat down on the wooden planks. He circled his arms around us both. "There are always some secrets in every relationship."

"She does have a point," Tiyah said.

Elijah shook his head. "Point or no, this is about trusting us to do what we need to do—in private. Besides, our pack would not feel comfortable changing in front of a non-werewolf."

"We can ask." Tiyah got up and sat behind him to massage his shoulders. He sank back, relaxing into her.

Our eyes met and she motioned for me to sit in his lap. I gladly draped myself across him, nestling my butt between his thighs. His hands immediately moved to my breasts, lifting and squeezing them. My head fell against his chest, watching Tiyah strain her body forward to kiss him while he stroked me.

"We like to wear ourselves out before a shift," she murmured around his mouth.

My breath hitched at that and the way he was handling my tits. Amazing. Just the right amount of pressure, like he was made just for me. Cupping one, he eased it from my tight corset until my nipple popped out. He broke his kiss with his wife to suck and tease me with his teeth and tongue. Under my ass, his hard cock pressed up, indicating how happy he was with the arrangement.

Tiyah switched positions, straddling both me and him. I almost squealed. They made me their Burgundy sandwich, my dream come true. She pressed her lips to mine and he ground himself into my backside, panting.

"My two beautiful women," he growled. "If polygamy were legal I'd marry you both."

What? Oh. My. God.

Tiyah pressed herself hard against me, grinding into me while I ground into Elijah.

A whistle from the dock brought us all out of our lust, fast.

"Can I join?" a man's voice rang out.

Tiyah leapt up, adjusting her suit.

The man ogled. "Nice titty."

Elijah was on his feet in a second, growling. "If you want to keep your balls, you will walk away. Fast."

"Aw, come on man, there's only one of you. Surely you can share."

"These are my women, get the hell away. Now."

The man took a step toward their boat. "If you didn't want to share, you shouldn't have been screwing them in plain sight."

As fast as I was, Elijah moved impossibly faster. Like we were in synch, I moved with him and was on the dock with the man's throat in a vice grip. Elijah stood next to me with his hands on his hips.

The man held his hands up, palms out. "Okay, okay, Jesus, tell her to let me go," he rasped.

Elijah smiled savagely. "Tell her yourself."

Flashing my fangs, I snarled, "If you want to live, you'll leave."

"I'm going," the man whispered, his eyes bulging.

I let go and the man fell down on the dock, then scrambled to get up.

My man put his arm around me. "If you ever look at either of my women again," he snarled, "she'll kill you."

The man ran down the dock without looking back.

"Hey man," a voice called over the jangle of the boat's bell.

We were all passed out together in their berth, legs and arms intertwined.

"Shit." Elijah jumped up and peeked out a porthole. The sun was low in the sky. "We don't have much time."

Tiyah and I scurried to put our clothes on while he went to the door.

"Been ravaging your wife again?" It was Jonas's voice.

"Something like that," Elijah said.

"You look like you just woke up," another male voice said.

"You ladies decent?" Elijah called out.

"Ladies? As in plural?" A woman's voice this time.

"Come in," Elijah said without answering.

"Burgundy's here too?" Jonas asked.

"Who's Burgundy?" The unknown male.

The group filed in while I stayed in their berth, Tiyah holding up her hand, indicating for me to wait there.

Everyone piled into the main compartment. I peeked my head around the wall briefly. There were two strangers with Jonas. Quickly I pulled back out of sight again, holding my breath.

My phone rang; it was Carter. I pressed the button to silence it.

"She's still here?" Jonas barked. "What the hell, Elijah? We have to set sail. Like now!"

Elijah sighed deeply. "I'm sorry to spring this on all of you, but Burgundy is our chosen mate."

"Our?" The woman's voice rang out.

"Elijah's and mine," Tiyah said.

Carter called again.

"Go ahead and take that if you need to Burg," Elijah called out.

"Hello," I answered my phone.

"Hey, where are you?" Carter asked.

"I'm with Eli and Tiyah."

"Is it safe?"

"I think so," I whispered. The group in the main cabin was speaking in hushed tones and I didn't want to disturb them.

"I'm at the V with Chrys. It's overflowing. Benedict had to turn people away."

"Because of the full moon?"

"Yeah, it's crazy. I had no idea how werewolf obsessed people were. There are humans camping out in the woods, hoping to catch a glimpse."

"You're kidding."

"Truth. I called to tell you. I think it's a good sign."

I had to agree. If this many people were into it, surely they'd want the werewolves to make a home here. When I hung up a few minutes later, I realized the boat was moving. With me on it.

Chapter Thirty-Nine

I waited in the berth until Tiyah came to get me, clasping my hand in hers. She tugged me gently into the main room. A tribunal?

The male and female I didn't know stood up and introduced themselves to me, shaking my hand. Melanie and Hale, who hen sat back down at the table together and held hands.

Elijah gestured for me to sit on the loveseat and I squeezed to the side to make room for him and Tiyah. Jonas wasn't there and I assumed he was the one maneuvering the boat.

"This is our pack." Eli motioned to the group. "And like Jonas, they don't understand our relationship, but . . ."

"We accept it," Melanie finished. "Any mate of

our pack is part of our pack. Welcome." She beamed at me.

"There's a lot more discussion to be had but not right now," Hale said, tapping his watch. "Elijah and Jonas have told us that you've advocated for our kind even before you knew about them and Tiyah. Is that correct?"

I nodded.

"And we understand that you're estranged from your father, partly because of the way he was trying to treat us?" Hale asked.

"Yes, that's true," I said.

"We're tired of running," Melanie said.

"I can understand that."

"Tiyah thought that if you were here to witness our change, you could report back to the others, letting them know that we *can* control ourselves," Melanie said.

"People fear what they don't understand," I said, "and I'm honored that you trust me enough to let me stay here." My heart rate had increased and I wondered if any of them could pick that up with their advanced senses.

"We don't," Hale said. "But we do trust our pack, and three of them are vouching for you. Let's hope you don't prove them wrong."

Tiyah squeezed my hand and I bit my tongue.

The boat's engine ceased its rumbled, followed by the loud splash of the anchor dropping.

"It's almost time," said Elijah. "Everyone on deck."

Melanie and Hale filed out of the cabin, Eli and Tiyah remaining behind.

"Here's what we're asking of you," Eli said.

"Anything," I replied, filled with a mixture of excitement and trepidation.

"We're trusting you enough to let you stay, but we ask that you remain inside. You can watch through the window after we've turned."

I nodded. "Of course, I would never watch the turning. My best friend's a shifter, I know how private it is."

Tiyah leaned in to peck my cheek. "I wish I could stay for a longer kiss." Her eyes were unguarded and fathomless, framed by those soft, mascara-less lashes.

Eli gave me that long kiss and then my lovers were gone, leaving me alone inside.

When the shifting started, I put my hands over my ears out of respect, but familiar sounds bled through. They were almost identical to the way Jared and Alec sounded when they shifted, like bones breaking and skin tearing.

Screaming floated by and then snarling and then . . . howling. Wow, they really did that? Chills ran over my skin; the howls were terrifying. I peeked through my fingers, then removed my hands entirely, pressing my face to the porthole. The creatures were mesmerizing. Thick hair and wolf bodies. It was obvious these were no ordinary wolves, though. They were too large for one, almost twice the size of a normal wolf, and their snouts were not quite as long. Two were gray, two brown and one was black. At first I couldn't tell who was who. But the black one was the largest and the first to howl. His teeth were huge, pointed and ripe for tearing flesh. Jonas, their leader.

More sharp teeth shone in the moonlight as they howled together, standing on two feet. Why had I expected them to look more wolf-like? They stood upright, and then as though they could hear my thoughts, they dropped to all fours. I watched, fascinated, as they circled one another, sniffing, like dogs.

I picked my lovers out next. Elijah was brown and Tiyah gray. Their eyes were darker than when they were humans but I could see a glimpse of their humanity. No other way to explain it. I simply knew, without a doubt, that these were my lovers.

Fascinated, I watched as a tongue shot out, lapping at another creature. Then they fell on each other in a pile of fur, teeth and tongues.

Instinctively, I leapt back. Were they fighting? I

remained quiet, listening to their growling and wailing. Peeking again, they were tumbling and turning until I realized they were engaged in some sort of sexual behavior. Well, that was one way to pass the time. *My* favorite way. Nice.

They were having werewolf sex and it was fascinating. They'd wanted me to watch this and my heart pounded with blood.

Chapter Forty

When I opened my eyes I was lying in the front berth, sandwiched between my lovers, all three of us covered with a blanket. The boat wasn't moving so either we were still anchored out at sea or we were back in the harbor.

I placed soft kisses on Eli's face and then on Tiyah's, their eyes opened in unison.

"Thank you," I murmured, "for letting me experience such an intimate moment. I've fallen hard for both of you. Madly, crazy hard."

Her lips curved upward and she closed her eyes, sighing deeply. Eli's arm wrapped around me and Tiyah, pulling us both closer to him.

"We love you too," he breathed.

"So much." She nestled her face into my hair.

Heaven. The scent of ripe peaches and deep sandalwood wafted over me.

My phone pinged on the nightstand and Eli reached for it, handing it to me lazily.

It was a text from Benedict. *They're in. The vote was unanimous.*

"*Hola, Mama.*" I opened my front door. "Did you have a good flight?" I leaned in to kiss her cheeks. We stood for a moment facing each other, neither of us daring to even breathe, and then she threw her arms around me, pulling me in tightly.

I looked behind her but she was alone. "Juan didn't want to come see me?"

"He's having a difficult time with your father leaving and didn't want to accidentally run into him. It was not an easy decision."

The disappointment must have shown on my face because my mother reached out and smoothed my hair, the way she used to when I was a little girl. I'd forgotten that. "Come in, please." I stood aside as she walked past me, her head swiveling from left to right.

I knew my house was a lot to take in and I tried to read her while she looked, slack jawed. When she finally turned back to me, her lips were curled into an enormous smile, which took me off guard. I unclenched hands I hadn't realized were twisted into my palms.

"I love the way you've decorated."

"Thank you." Wow, in a flash, my boho Moroccan theme was redeemed.

"What are those boxes?" she pointed to the far wall. "New things?"

"No." I shook my head, letting a breath of air escape. "I'm packing up."

"What? Why?"

"We can't afford to live here anymore." So much had happened, I wasn't sure what to tell her or how.

"But, Maria . . ."

I stiffened.

"I'm sorry. Burgundy." She offered me a smile. I took it. "I thought you owned the house, no?"

"No." I clenched my jaw.

"But when you moved here, I insisted that your father buy it for you. I don't understand."

It had been my mother's idea all along? Figured. "It turns out he financed it, keeping it in his name so that he could pull the plug when I displeased him."

"*Bastardo*," she growled.

My eyebrows shot up. She rarely cussed. "Do you want to sit in the kitchen and have some tea?" She followed me in and perched on the edge of a wooden chair. "I don't have your favorite but I do have licorice."

"Muy bien." She looked down at her hands. "Is your father still here? With that woman?"

I poured hot water into two mugs. "No, they left."

"He's not speaking to you?"

"I'm not speaking to him. Our relationship is over."

"I'm so sorry. Are you okay? Is there anything I can do?"

Her response surprised me. I don't know what I was expecting. An *I told you so* or *what did you expect?* "You're doing it. You're here." Either she had changed or I had. Maybe it was both of us?

She waited, silently, wearing a look of pure empathy.

"He's not who I thought he was," I blurted.

"I know what you mean." She sighed. "It's easiest for us to lie to ourselves, no?"

"I guess so, yeah." I brought her tea over and took the seat beside her.

"You're sad?"

"I'm sad that I never got to have a loving, caring father. Instead, I got someone whose love was always conditional. But right now, surprisingly, I'm also relieved. I wanted so hard for him to accept me that I became someone I didn't like. I became like him. I don't want to do that anymore."

"But you aren't like him. And even if you think you were, each day we can strive to be better than we were the day before."

I got up, pacing around the kitchen. She radiated such peace while I was still struggling to process everything. "How can you not be angry at him, Mom?"

She shrugged. "I am, a little."

"He gets a fucking do-over. Hervé Rosales gets to reinvent himself with an entirely new family."

"Sweetheart. Who knows what is in his heart and mind? I'm devastated at the loss of my marriage, yes. But I'd rather not be living under his tyranny anymore."

"Why'd you stay for so long?" I had to know.

"For you and Juan. I couldn't support either of you on my own and I wanted you to have the best of everything. I thought . . ." She looked away, bloody tears forming in her eyes.

I reached out and took her hand. "What is it, Mama?"

"I'm so sorry." Red tears spilled onto her ruddy cheeks. "*Chica*, I love you so much. I've always wanted what was best for you and I thought that was letting you think your father was a good man, a better person than me. Yet in the end I failed you."

"You didn't fail me, but you did fail yourself." I got up and got her one of my black handkerchiefs.

Our relationship had been strained for so long. It felt like she'd rarely hugged me growing up, or even spoken to me. Like I'd been invisible to her. But how much of that reticence on her part had been because of my father? How much had he driven a wedge between us, made us think we were in competition for his love, so we'd try harder for his affection? My mother was supposed to love me unconditionally, but Hervé Rosales had poisoned those around him for decades. Maybe without him, my mother and I could have a second chance.

"I've been seeing a therapist since he left. She's helped me figure out so much. I wanted to formally apologize, it's why I'm here."

"I appreciate your courage." I felt closer to my mother than I had in a long, *long* time. Maybe the silver lining to everything would be our mended relationship. "We all make mistakes."

Just then, Jared bounded into the kitchen, back from his walk with Rex.

"Mama!" he cried out, throwing his arms around her and almost knocking her out of her chair.

"Jaredito," she crooned happily into the crook of his neck, her chair sideways.

I loved seeing him with my mother. I had worked so hard for so long to make my life here, to make my chosen friends my support group. My family. And now here was my mother, so openly accepting of them. I was losing the house my father had provided me, but maybe I was regaining my mother.

Chapter Forty-One

Dancing with Tiyah eased my mind. Both men and women approached us to stuff bills into our G-strings but we hardly noticed them. We were too focused on each other and Elijah. He was standing to the side of the stage, riveted, alternately licking his lips and smiling. After our set, we would sequester ourselves to a back room so Elijah could ravage us both. The three of us had explored our sexual relationship further, but it was the emotional component that shined through in the movements between Tiyah and myself. We could read each other like braille and had no problem improvising a sequence, one of us finishing the other's moves like old married couples finishing each other's sentences. Well, if that old married couple was showing off for their mate.

The problems at home had sloughed off. I'd packed up all of my belongings and moved them into storage. My lovers had asked me to move in with them on the boat, and while I loved their boat, which we'd christened "Wolfie," it was too small for the three of us. Where would I put my clothes?

Instead, I was looking for a rental. Jared and Alec had already found a house to rent; Chrys and Carter were bunking there for now. They hadn't decided on anything long-term yet, but whatever happened now, Casa Mañana was gone. The loss of my dream home hurt less than the loss of my roommates. Living without them was painful but, I reminded myself, the only constant in life was change. Another chapter closed to start a brand new book. My future with my chosen mates.

As I whipped Tiyah across the stage, then turned back to the audience, I caught sight of Amber waving and smiling from the back. She was sitting at a table with two gorgeous male suitors, each one draping a hand behind her chair. My heart swelled for her.

When Tiyah slid back into my arms, I twirled us sideways again to give Elijah a better view. An overwhelming sense of peace and acceptance flowed over me.

No longer alone and lost at sea, my lovers represented the home I'd always yearned for. They were my private island, my lighthouse on the shore, my welcoming harbor.

Tiyah and I finished our dance with nothing on but tiny G-strings and pasties. The din of the appreciative audience faded as I grabbed my woman's deliciously sweaty body and pressed my mouth to hers.

Entwined on the stage, we made out, oblivious and uncaring, our bodies crushed together, hands exploring curves with soft caresses under the burning lights. Hands reached out from the audience, but there was no more room in our G-strings, so they littered the stage with bills.

We finally broke our kiss and smiled out into the crowd to our standing ovation. Elijah approached us with robes and draped them over our shoulders, kissing each of us in turn.

He escorted us to a table in the back.

"We have something to ask you," he said as they flanked me.

"Shoot."

"We want to move off the boat and get an apartment with you." Tiyah reached for my hand, clasping it tightly. Elijah took my other hand and brought it to his lips.

"That sounds perfect." I smiled at them both. "I trust you two with my future. What matters to me is that we're all together. Home isn't a place—it's not something that can be bought or sold, or held over one's head as a conditional, material object. Home is what lives inside." I pressed a hand to my chest.

"We know what losing Casa Mañana has meant to you," Tiyah said softly.

"I think I named my house Casa Mañana because happiness was always just out of reach. I was always striving for tomorrow. But that's moot now that I have you two. Today, my dreams have come true."

My lovers and I embraced, and all memories of my prior loneliness were swept completely out to sea.

The End

Also by Chloe Adler

Want to read Iphigenia's Story? Grab the boxed set, Tales from the Edge, beginning with Distant Light!

Fancy a FREE Novella? Fire and Fangs is a sexy, enemies to lovers, multiple partner paranormal with sword-crossing. Join Chloe's newsletter to download it here: https://BookHip.com/QFGLCWZ

Looking for more electrifying reads that will leave you spellbound? Look no further than one (or all) of Chloe Adler's five sizzling paranormal romance series, totaling seventeen delectable books!

A slow burn multiple partner saga promising a hint of darkness:

Tales from the Edge starting with Distant Light **which follows Iphigenia**, the sweet, empathic witch and her four loves including an alpha dragon shifter.

Chronicles of Tara starting with Synergist, a fantasy reverse

harem with fae. Tara tells the story of Amaya, an unlikely heroine and her five enigmatic heroes.

Fast Burn Darker Multiple Partner Books:

Destiny Chronicles beginning with Descent stars Sydney, a defiant sex worker and her five provocative heroes.

Danger after Dark beginning with Paris (but these can easily be read out of order). Each novella follows a different heroine traveling through Europe and their three dangerous heroes.

Follow Chloe on your favorite social media platform or drop her a line, she would love to hear from you!

- Instagram - @chloeadlerauthor
- TikTok - @chloeadlerauthor
- Facebook - facebook.com/groups/523600161317601
- Bookbub - bookbub.com/profile/chloe-adler
- Amazon - www.amazon.com/stores/Chloe-Adler/author/B06ZZ838HR

- Goodreads - goodreads.com/author/show/16722267.Chloe_Adler
- Pinterest: pinterest.com/ChloeAdlerAuthor/

I am thankful for the trust you place in me as an author, for embracing the vulnerable and authentic parts of my storytelling.
XO - Chloe